"You're In My Room."

Tess gazed up at him, drowsy and confused.

"When I knocked and you didn't answer, I thought something had happened to you," Ben said. "I shouldn't have come in uninvited."

No, he shouldn't have, but Tess couldn't seem to be angry with him. Anyway, it wasn't as if he'd never seen her in bed before. In bed *and* naked.

He moved to the door. "Good night, Tess. Sleep well."

She lay awake a long time, counting the reasons staying here was a good idea, so she could forget the reasons it wasn't.

Because if Ben kept touching her so tenderly, and looking at her with those bedroom eyes, she was going to do something stupid, like sleep with him again. Then she'd wind up doing something even *more* stupid.

Like fall in love.

Dear Reader,

As a young and naive newly wed mother (emphasis on the words *young and naive*), I used to place an awful lot of importance on making money and buying stuff. I just took for granted that every year our income would climb and someday in the not-so-distant future we would have our dream house, expensive cars, designer clothes and enough money to live comfortably the rest of our lives.

Remember, young and naive.

Needless to say, it didn't happen that way. A bad economy, chronic illness and plain old dumb luck have taught me many important lessons over the past eighteen years.

If given the chance, would I go back and change things? If I could start my life over, what would I do different?

Not a thing.

Because despite the fact that my life didn't turn out exactly as I'd planned all those years ago, I'm happy. I have a roof over my head, a husband who completes me, three great kids and a career I absolutely love. What more could I possibly ask for?

I thought it would be interesting to take a man who has everything money could buy, and is so devastated by loss, he has to be reminded that it is the simple things that make life worth living.

Hope you enjoy it!

Michelle Celmer

MICHELLE CELMER

The Millionaire's Pregnant Mistress

Published by Silhouette Books
America's Publisher of Contemporary Romance

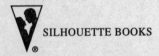 SILHOUETTE BOOKS

ISBN-13: 978-0-373-76739-7
ISBN-10:   0-373-76739-0

THE MILLIONAIRE'S PREGNANT MISTRESS

Copyright © 2006 by Michelle Celmer

This edition published by arrangement with Harlequin Books S.A.

® and TM are trademarks of Harlequin Books S.A., used under license.
Trademarks indicated with ® are registered in the United States Patent
and Trademark Office, the Canadian Trade Marks Office and in other
countries.

Visit Silhouette Books at www.eHarlequin.com

Printed in U.S.A.

Books by Michelle Celmer

Silhouette Desire

Playing by the Baby Rules #1566
The Seduction Request #1626
Bedroom Secrets #1656
Round-the-Clock Temptation #1683
House Calls #1703
The Millionaire's Pregnant Mistress #1739

Silhouette Intimate Moments

Running on Empty #1342
Out of Sight #1398

MICHELLE CELMER

Bestselling author Michelle Celmer lives in southeastern Michigan with her husband, their three children, two dogs and two cats. When she's not writing or busy being a mom, you can find her in the garden or curled up with a romance novel. And if you twist her arm real hard, you can usually persuade her into a day of power shopping.

Michelle loves to hear from readers. Visit her Web site at: www.michellecelmer.com, or write her at P.O Box 300, Clawson, MI 48017.

Though they aren't likely to ever read this, I dedicate this book to my dogs Spunky, Rocko and Combat, and my cats PeeWee and Bubba. They love me unconditionally, keep me company when I'm lonely and always make me smile.

One

In her twenty-four years, Tess McDonald had made her share of bad judgment calls, but this one topped them all. All of her life she'd been determined not to turn out like her mother, but here she was, making the same stupid mistakes. Maybe it was destiny.

Or just dumb luck.

She stared up at the sprawling structure of marble and granite. Dark and foreboding under overcast, gloomy skies, it loomed before her like a castle out of a modern-day fairy tale. An enchanted castle where nothing was as it seemed and monsters lay in wait, ready to devour unsuspecting maidens. And what fairy tale would be complete without an embittered, cagey prince? A loner afflicted by some disfiguring curse, set free only by love in its purest form.

But Tess had abandoned the mystical for the practical a long time ago. Fairy tales weren't real. There were no princes—cursed or otherwise—no enchanted castles and the only monster she knew was still living with her mother back in Utah.

She climbed the wide marble steps to the front door, and lifted a reluctant hand—*come on Tess, just do it*—and forced herself to press the bell. The hollow ring penetrated the massive, intricately carved double doors, kicking her heart into a frantic beat. Seconds ticked by as she waited for someone to answer. Seconds that felt like hours. When she'd almost convinced herself no one was home, the door opened.

She'd expected a maid or a butler, one in full uniform of course—possibly looking like Lurch from the Addams Family. Instead it was Ben, looking much like he had when they'd met.

Mysteriously and intriguingly dark.

His raven hair lay at his collar in silky waves and heavy lidded bedroom eyes in the darkest, richest shade of brown, studied her. Everything about him reeked of prestige and wealth, from the expensive looking black cashmere sweater and custom tailored slacks, to the tantalizing scent of his cologne.

She felt the same shiver of excitement as she had when she'd caught him staring at her from across the bar that night. Their eyes had met, and the heat pen-

etrating in the dark, bottomless depths made her heart
go berserk with anticipation.

The way it was now.

He hadn't said a word. He'd just held out his hand
in silent invitation and she'd taken it. He'd led her to
the dance floor and when he pulled her into his arms,
pressed her to the lean length of his body, she melted
against him. Then he'd dipped his head and brushed
his lips over hers.

Now, there were kisses, and there were *kisses*.

Kissing Ben had felt like two pieces of a puzzle
locking together in a perfect fit. Her knees had gone
weak, and the room had spun around her like a
carousel. She knew in that instant that she would sleep
with him. It wasn't even a conscious decision. It was
just something she had to do. An opportunity she
would regret for the rest of her life if she let it pass.

She also knew that he was just interested in one
night. The, I'm-not-looking-for-a-relationship line
he fed her between kisses in the elevator on the way
up to his room had been a big tip-off. She'd never
expected to see him again.

Considering the look on his face now, neither had
he.

She knew she should say something, but she
couldn't seem to make her mouth work. All she could
do was stare, wondering if he knew who she was. If
he remembered her. If he was wondering how she'd
managed to track him down. She'd never been one
to read the tabloids and she didn't have cable televi-

sion so it had been weeks later that she'd learned from the girls at work who he really was.

What he'd been hiding.

He wedged his shoulder in the doorjamb and folded his arms over his chest, looking her up and down, those dark eyes putting a chink in the man-resistant armor she wore these days.

"And here I thought you'd been abducted by aliens," he finally said, in that velvety dark-chocolate voice.

Okay, so he did remember her.

He wasn't really going to pretend she'd wronged him somehow, was he? To stay the night in his room would have only been delaying the inevitable. The morning brush-off. The *gee-it-was-nice, have-a-good-life* speech men like him were notorious for.

At the time, she didn't think her heart could take that, because she had fallen stupidly and completely in love with Ben that night.

"You weren't looking for a relationship," she reminded him.

His eyes narrowed. The same bottomless pools she'd found so entrancing that night. How could she have known what he'd really been hiding behind that dark exterior?

The smoldering look in his eyes burned hotter. "I'm still not looking for a relationship."

"I just came to talk. Can I come inside?"

Though he looked hesitant, he held the door open wider and stepped back, all but disappearing into the dark interior.

The rubber soles of her work shoes squeaked on the marble floor as she stepped inside the cavernous foyer, and hazy darkness swallowed her like a hungry beast. As her eyes adjusted to the dim light, oddly shaped, ominous shadows crept soundlessly around her like restless spirits.

You don't believe in spooks, she reminded herself.

The door closed behind her with a thud that bounced off the walls and echoed up the cathedral ceiling. Ben simply stood there, towering over her, arms folded over his chest, biceps straining against the sleeves of his shirt, his face hidden in shadow. His intimidating size, ropes of lean, corded muscle, were part of what had intrigued her that night, what had drawn her to him. As if she hadn't learned her lesson so many times before. Dark angsty men were nothing but trouble.

But, boy they could be fun for a night or two.

He may have been dark and reserved in the bar, but under the covers she'd never had a more attentive, exciting or *imaginative* lover. It was all coming back now. How alive and beautiful he'd made her feel.

And why she'd run like hell in the middle of the night.

What he didn't know is that he'd given her a gift. The piece of her that had always been missing, even if she hadn't realized it. For the first time in her life she had a purpose. She wasn't alone. And for that she owed him everything.

That included an explanation.

True, the timing couldn't have been worse, but that didn't mean she wasn't happy. And scared of course. This would change everything.

She'd considered not telling him. Odds are he never would have found out. They didn't exactly run in the same social circles. In fact, she had worked so many hours since moving here, she wasn't even part of a social circle. And after everything he'd been through in the past year, well, he probably would have been better off left in the dark.

And considering the lack of light in here, that was exactly where he preferred to be.

She thought she could handle the burden alone, but as hard as she'd tried, her best efforts just weren't cutting it anymore. She needed his help. And since there was no easy way to say it, to soften the blow, she decided it was best to just get it out.

She took a deep breath and held her chin high. "I just thought you should know that I'm pregnant and you're the father."

Her words hit Ben like a sucker punch.

For months now he'd considered going back to the resort bar in the hopes that she would be there. That they could reconnect. Something inside him had changed that night with her. He'd begun living again.

But this he'd never expected.

She may have acted as if she hadn't known who he was that night in the resort, but clearly he'd been set up.

How could he have been so stupid?

He knew exactly how, and why now, months later, he still felt that tug of longing when she stood in his foyer. She'd been the first woman he'd connected with since the crash. The only one who had been able to make him forget the pain.

He used to believe that his heart had died along with his wife and unborn son, but something had clicked between himself and Tess that night.

Maybe it was because she was so different from Jeanette. Slim and angular and schoolgirl pretty to his wife's lush figure and exotic beauty. She'd looked so petite and nymphlike. Sweet and innocent.

What a joke.

He never should have left the house that night, but the idea of spending the holidays in solitude had forced him out of his self-imposed isolation. He should have known what was up when he woke the next morning alone. Yes, it was true he told her he wasn't looking for a relationship, but he hadn't asked her to leave, either. He thought there had been a connection.

Apparently, he'd thought wrong.

He wondered how many other men she'd picked up in that bar. How many she'd used. And why she'd picked him to seal the deal. Because he was vulnerable? Or was it his bank balance?

And to think that he'd been *this close* to falling in love with her.

"You neglected to mention that you worked at the resort," he said. She hadn't told him much of anything about herself. Not that he'd asked. He hadn't been looking for conversation, just a sweet, warm body to lose himself in. Kind of like a Christmas present to himself. By the time he realized he wanted more, she'd already disappeared.

She lifted her chin and looked him in the eye. "We didn't spend a whole lot of time getting to know each other."

"Actually, I thought we got to know each other rather...*intimately.*"

Tess bit her lip and her cheeks flushed bright pink. It would have been charming if he believed it were anything but an act.

"Maybe you don't remember, but we used protection," he said, sure that she would come up with some creative excuse why the condom had failed. All three of them, or had it been four?

She didn't. "Believe me, I was just as surprised as you are. I didn't plan this, either."

"Let's say it is mine. What do you want from me?" Like he didn't already know. She probably had a long list of demands. Would she expect him to marry her? Did she think they would settle down together and play house? Or maybe she was looking for a break into acting.

She wouldn't be the first who'd tried to use him for his connections.

She lowered her eyes to the floor, looking genuinely humbled. Give the girl an Oscar, she was one hell of an actress. "I need your help. I thought I could do this alone, but with the doctor bills and all the things I need for the baby…"

Just as he suspected.

"I want a paternity test," he told her. "Before I give you a penny, I need to know if this really is my baby."

Tess nodded, thankful he wasn't going to make her beg. Her mother had struggled for years to make Tess's wealthy father own up to his responsibility and pay child support. Tess had been sure Ben would fight her tooth and nail.

"I figured you would. I've already talked to my doctor about it. She said they can do the test next week, when I go in for my ultrasound."

"Fine. I'll contact my attorney."

"If you want, you could come with me," she said, figuring it was the least she could do. It was his baby as much as hers. Maybe they could reach some sort of accord, find some middle ground and maybe even learn not to resent each other.

Maybe they could even be friends.

"Come where?" he asked.

"To the appointment. To see the baby."

Something dark and unsettling flashed across his face. He closed in on her, his eyes sparking with anger. "Let's get something straight. If this is really my child, I'll see that it's taken care of, but I can't be a part of its life."

She took a step back and bumped into the door. He moved forward, boxing her in. If he was trying to intimidate her, it was working.

And he knew it.

"Why so nervous?" he said, easing even nearer, bracing his hands on either side of her head. Black hair framed his face, settling it deeper into the shadows, but she could still see his eyes—dark and penetrating pinned on her face. And so cold it made her shiver. "You didn't mind being this close that night in my room. In fact, I was under the impression you rather enjoyed it."

She glared up at him, refusing to be the one who backed down. She'd almost forgotten how beautiful he was. Beautiful in a completely masculine, testosterone driven way of course. But that was to be expected being the product of two gorgeous Academy Award winning actors.

He smelled good, too. The scent of his cologne and sheer male heat swirled through the narrow space between them. He smelled expensive and refined and…

My God, was she actually getting turned on by this he-man macho crap? It had to be the pregnancy hormones making her feel so loopy.

After that night with Ben she had forever sworn off men like him. They were nothing but trouble. If she ever did date again—and that was a big *if*—she was going to find herself a quiet, average, boring guy. She'd take safe and unexciting over sizzling and sexy any day.

She poked the solid mass of his chest with her index finger, feeling his body-heat soak through the silky softness of his sweater, enjoying the look of surprise on his face.

"You must think pretty highly of yourself if you believe I would want a relationship with you. Just like you, I went up to your room expecting one night. Go ahead and pin the blame on me if it eases your guilty conscience, but this is as much your fault as it is mine. I wasn't in that room alone. If I recall correctly, you *rather enjoyed it,* too. And need I remind you that you were the one with the condoms? How do I know you didn't do this on purpose? Maybe you get some sort of depraved thrill knocking up unsuspecting women. For all I know, you have illegitimate children all over the place."

His expression shifted and he looked almost... wounded.

Was it possible she'd hurt his feelings? That he actually *had* feelings?

Ben dropped his hands from beside her head and backed away, his face somber. He looked so...sad. The brief charge of satisfaction hissed away like a deflating balloon.

"May as well take off your jacket and get comfortable," he said. "We have a lot to discuss."

Ben sat at his desk and ripped open the envelope his lawyer had messaged over. With a heavy heart, he read the results of the paternity test she'd taken last week. The wounds that had begun to heal in the year since his son's death ripped open and grief twisted his insides.

Tess had been telling the truth. The baby was his.

If he had been able to talk Jeanette out of taking the trip to Tahoe while he wrapped up postproduction on his last film, she and his son would be alive. Even the doctor had said it was late in her pregnancy to be flying. Ben should have insisted, but when Jeanette wanted something she usually got it.

He would never forgive himself for letting them down, and he wouldn't let it happen again. This baby was his, whether he wanted it or not. He would see that it was taken care of and raised properly.

In his son's honor, he wouldn't let anything bad happen to this child.

"I take it the news wasn't what you'd hoped."

He looked up to find Mildred Smith, his housekeeper, watching him from the doorway. Any other of his employees would have been fired for insinuating themselves into his business, but Mrs. Smith had been with his family since before Ben was born. It had only been natural to hire her when his parents moved permanently to Europe three years ago. She'd been with him those horrible months after the crash and had nursed him through the worst of it. She was more like family than hired help. More of a mother to him than his own mother had ever been.

"It's mine," he told her.

"What do you plan to do now?" she asked.

The only thing he could do. "I'm going to make sure she and the baby are safe. I'll bring her here to live with us until it's born."

"You know nothing about this girl." Her tone was

stern, bordering on cold, but that was just her way. He knew she cared deeply for him. The past year hadn't been easy for her, either. Though Mrs. Smith had never cared for Ben's wife, the loss had hit her hard.

"I don't know her, which is exactly the reason I need to keep her close. That's my child she's carrying."

The one thing he didn't get, that didn't make sense about this whole situation, was why she'd waited so long to tell him. According to her due date, she had to be close to sixteen weeks pregnant. Meaning she'd known she was pregnant for at least a couple of months already.

He was sure she had her reasons.

He found the number Tess had jotted down on a slip of paper. It had been sitting there on his desk, taunting him for days. He hadn't yet written it in his book, on the slim hope it was all a mistake. Since her visit last week, all communication had been through his attorney. Now it was time to make his position clear. Face-to-face.

"Suppose she doesn't want to live here?" Mrs. Smith asked. "What then?"

He gave her a look, one that said he didn't anticipate that being an issue. "You think a girl like that, with a menial job at the resort and next to nothing to her name, would pass up the opportunity to live in luxury? I know her kind. She'll take whatever I have to offer."

Two

"Absolutely not! There is no way I'm moving in with you." All that Hollywood fame must have gone to Ben's head if he thought he could boss her around. He hadn't even asked. Instead he'd issued an order.

He sat casually behind his enormous desk like a king on his throne addressing his royal subjects. The only thing missing was a scepter and crown.

And tights—which she had to admit would be well worth seeing.

Instead he wore black again. Black shirt, black slacks. Did he own a single article of clothing in color?

Tess turned to see if the stern woman who had let her in was still standing in the doorway listening.

Thankfully she wasn't.

Ben, Tess could handle. At least, she was going to give it a valiant effort. His housekeeper on the other hand—Lurch's twin sister—gave her a serious case of the creeps.

"I have an apartment," she said. "I don't need or want to live here."

"I didn't need or want a child, yet one is being forced on me."

"I did not make this baby all by myself," she reminded him. "Besides, what has that got to do with where I live?"

"You live in a disreputable part of town. It's not safe."

"I do the best I can." Not everyone was born with a silver spoon in their mouth—or in his case, an entire service for twelve. She was quite sure he had no concept of what it was like to struggle, to live on canned spaghetti and Wonder Bread until the next payday.

"If geography is such a problem for you, we can compromise. If you help me out financially, I can get a place in a part of town you deem as safe. Then we'll both be happy."

"Not acceptable. I need you here."

"As I said, I don't want to live here."

"Shall I send someone over to help you pack?" he asked, as if she hadn't just *emphatically* stated that she *would not* be moving.

She normally had interminable patience, but this guy was pushing all her buttons. "Are you hearing impaired? I said that I'm not moving into your house. That's final."

He went on as though she hadn't spoken. "I also think it would be best if you quit your job. As a maid, you probably work with harmful cleaning solvents, and heavy lifting must be involved. It could be damaging for the baby."

Whoa. Someone had serious control issues. Did he really think she would allow herself to become totally dependent on him? She'd been on her own since she was sixteen. She knew how to take care of herself, and she would take care of her baby. She just needed a little help—emphasis on *little.* A couple hundred bucks a month to help cover her extra expenses.

She glanced at the crystal tumbler filled with some sort of amber colored alcohol sitting on his desk. Warning bells clanged like crazy through her brain. She'd heard rumors from the other employees at the resort that he'd become a reclusive alcoholic since he'd lost his wife. The reclusive part she believed, the alcoholic part she'd only hoped wasn't true. Looks like she might have been wrong.

Not that everyone who drank was an alcoholic, but she wasn't taking any chances.

"I'm not quitting my job. I'll give you weekly updates on my condition if it will make you feel better, but that's it."

"That reminds me," he said. "I've picked an obstetrician I'd like you to see. He's the best in the area."

And it just kept getting weirder. Now he wanted

to pick her doctor? Next he would be telling her how to dress, and what to eat.

"I already have a doctor I'm comfortable with that takes my insurance," she told him.

"Expense isn't an issue."

"It is for me, since I'm the one paying for it."

He folded his arms across his chest and leaned back in his chair. His face was partially hidden in shadow, but if she could see it, she was sure he would look annoyed.

It was so darned dark in here.

"What are you, a vampire? Could we maybe open some drapes? Turn on a light or two?"

He unfolded his arms, leaned forward and switched on the desk lamp. Yep, he looked annoyed all right.

"You mean to make this as difficult as possible, don't you?" he asked.

Was he kidding? "*I'm* being difficult? You're not the one whose life is going to drastically change. You don't have to suffer the morning sickness and the weight gain and the stretch marks. And let's not forget hemorrhoids and heartburn and hours of hard labor. The day you can do all that for me, I'll let you start calling the shots. Until then, this is my body and my baby and I will go to whichever doctor I choose, and live wherever the heck I want. Is that clear?"

"If you don't cooperate I could fight you for custody. I have unlimited financial resources."

She knew he was desperate when he started tossing around legal threats.

"I've done my homework. I've got the numbers of half a dozen high profile bleeding heart attorneys who would just love to handle a case like mine pro bono."

She could swear she saw a hint of amusement in his eyes. "Would you really want to put yourself through that? Agree to my terms and I'll grant you full custody and adequate financial assistance to have you living in luxury for the rest of your life."

She took a deep, calming breath. "Apparently you're not hearing what I'm saying. I don't want to live in luxury. I want a *little* help. Got it?"

He stared up at her, a vague smile curling his lips.

She propped her hands on her hips and glared at him. "I fail to see what it is about this situation you find amusing."

He leaned back in his chair, gazing up at her. "I was just thinking about that night in the resort."

Oh great, now did he think sex would be a part of the deal? "What about it?"

"I knew there was a reason I liked you."

Now he *liked* her? That didn't make any sense.

"You are the most stubborn, self-centered, *confusing* person I have ever met," she said, and his grin widened. She never imagined a man so dark and sexy could look so…cute.

Cute? What was she thinking? He wasn't cute. He was a big pain in the neck.

She flung her hands up. "Fine, don't help me.

Because frankly, it isn't worth the trouble. The baby and I will manage without you."

She turned to leave and was halfway to the door when she heard him call, "Tess, wait."

No way. She was through arguing about this. She and the baby would make it without him. She wasn't sure how, but she would manage.

She made it to the door and had her hand on the knob when she heard him say, "Please, stay."

She reluctantly turned back to him.

"I know there has to be a way we can make this work."

"Unless you're willing to compromise, I don't see how."

"I am." He gestured to the chair across from his desk. "Please, sit."

Because he said please, she crossed the room and took a seat.

"Tell me what works for you, then we'll figure something out."

"You're serious?"

"Absolutely."

"First I have to ask, why the change of heart? Why are you willing to compromise now, when fifteen minutes ago you were being an ogre?"

He wasn't insulted by the observation, in fact, he smiled. "Fifteen minutes ago I thought I knew who you were."

"And now?"

"Now I realize I was wrong."

* * *

Tess prayed silently the way she did every morning as her old junker chugged its way up the mountain to the staff parking lot behind the resort. It had stalled twice on the way here. Once she'd flooded the engine and had to wait several minutes, holding up traffic, before it would turn over again.

Her carburetor was terminally ill, but it would be at least three or four months before she had the money saved to replace it. And that was if she did the work herself—which she was pretty sure she could manage given the time to figure it out. She'd blown her entire savings plus a week's groceries on a gas pump last month. The co-pay for her monthly doctor visits and prenatal vitamins was eating up the rest of her extra cash.

The downside to residing in a resort town was the astronomical cost of living. If she skipped grocery shopping again on Sunday, that would shave a week off her expenses, but the doctor had already expressed concern that she wasn't gaining enough weight, and a healthy diet was critical for a healthy pregnancy.

She'd spent the last few days thinking about Ben's offer. As far as she could tell, when she'd threatened to leave, he finally realized she was telling the truth. That the pregnancy was an accident and she wasn't after his money. Though for the life of her, she still didn't understand why it was so important that he have her living in his house. But when she stopped to think about it, there was no reason why she absolutely shouldn't live there. She would have her own suite and could come and go as she pleased.

Everything he'd had to offer sounded pretty good, except for one thing. Despite every other concession he'd made, he still insisted she quit her job.

Tess couldn't remember a time when she hadn't had some sort of job. Babysitting, delivering papers, stocking shelves at the party store—anything to earn a little extra spending cash. And later, hard work had been a way out of the hellhole that was her stepdad's house.

If she quit working now, what would she do for money? She already felt uncomfortable taking things from Ben. But to be totally dependent on him?

Frankly, she was scared. What if she gave up her job, then found out he was some kind of creep or weirdo? She'd be stuck, because she seriously doubted anyone would be jumping at the chance to hire a pregnant woman.

She'd told him to give her a few days to think about it, but she still wasn't sure what to do.

She pulled her car into a spot at the back of the employee lot, glanced at her watch, and cursed under her breath. She was ten minutes late.

Hopping from the car, she bolted for the back entrance. Olivia Montgomery, the owner of the resort, ruled like a foreign dictator, expecting one hundred and ten percent from her employees. Tardiness was not acceptable. And because of her temperamental carburetor, this was Tess's third time in two weeks.

Tess shoved her way through the door and headed to the employee locker room behind the kitchen. As she turned the corner, her heart sank when she saw the morning shift manager standing next to her locker waiting for her.

"I'm sorry I'm late," she said. "Car trouble."

His sour expression was tarter than usual. She was convinced the guy sucked lemons for breakfast. "Mrs. Montgomery would like a word with you."

Oh, swell. Getting chewed out by her boss was not her favorite way to start the day.

She shoved her jacket and purse into her locker and headed for Mrs. Montgomery's office, where the secretary greeted her with a sympathetic smile. "Go on in, she's waiting for you."

Tess opened the door and stepped inside the lush office. Her boss was on the phone, but gestured to the chair across from her desk, her expression unreadable.

She spoke for several minutes, then said goodbye to the person on the line, hung up the phone and turned to Tess.

Tess had learned that the best thing to do in a situation like this was to shelve her pride and take responsibility for her actions. "I'm very sorry for being late. I know it's unacceptable. I swear it won't happen again."

Her boss very calmly folded her hands atop her desk. "This is the third time in two weeks, Tess."

"I know, and I'm sorry."

"Well then, you can make it up by working a few

extra shifts this week," she said in that condescending, *I'm God and you're a peon* tone. "We have several people out with the flu."

Tess was already working over fifty hours a week. She'd been suffering a chronic backache and swollen knees from being on her feet too long, and her bad ankle had been stiff and sore. It also seemed that no matter how many hours she slept, she woke feeling exhausted. But she knew that if she didn't work the extra hours Mrs. Montgomery would find a reason to fire her. She knew Tess was pregnant, and that in several months she would be eligible for paid maternity leave.

She'd been looking for a reason to let Tess go.

And because of that, Tess had been working her tail off at a job that she quite frankly despised, for far less money than she deserved. Didn't she *deserve* a break? Hadn't she *earned* it?

She thought about Ben's enormous house and what it would be like to live there. What it would be like to not have to get up at 5 a.m. and drag herself to work. To stay up late watching movies and eating popcorn. To sleep until noon. How it would feel to relax and enjoy her pregnancy.

So maybe she wouldn't have a lot of extra spending money. So what? She was used to getting by on a tight budget.

But if she did this, that would be it, she would be stuck with Ben for five long months. Although, if she had to be *stuck* with someone, she could have done a lot worse.

"Well?" Mrs. Montgomery said tightly, expecting an answer.

"No," Tess said. "I'm afraid I can't do that."

Her boss's eyes narrowed. "I'm afraid you don't have a choice."

That wasn't true. For the first time in her life, Tess actually *did* have a choice.

What it all came down to was, what was best for her child? She grew up with nothing. Ben had everything. She wanted something in between for her baby.

If she accepted Ben's offer, the baby would never want for life's basic necessities, never feel threatened or abused. Her child would go to good schools and get a college education, would have all the opportunities she never had.

Ben could give them that, if she just had a little faith.

She still wasn't one hundred percent sure she could trust him, but she was so sick of feeling achy and tired and overworked. Maybe it was time she took a chance on him, the way he'd taken a chance on her.

She flashed her boss a smile, feeling that, for the first time in months, maybe she was doing the right thing. "I do have a choice, Mrs. Montgomery. And I choose to quit."

Three

"Benjamin, I'm sorry to interrupt, but there's someone here to see you."

Ben looked up from the computer screen to find Mrs. Smith standing in his office doorway. She opened the door wider and behind her stood Tess.

Her cheeks were pink from the cold and her eyes bright. She was dressed in a denim skirt and a fuzzy olive sweater that was just tight enough to reveal her stomach was no longer flat. She looked good. In spite of himself, he smiled.

He couldn't deny he was happy to see her. For reasons he probably shouldn't be.

He rose from his seat. "You're back."

She nodded and flashed him a tentative smile. "I'm back."

Mrs. Smith shot Ben a stern look. One that said she wasn't crazy about this arrangement—which she'd made clear on more than one occasion in the past few days—and she still thought he was making a mistake. Then she stepped out and shut the door behind her.

"I take it you've made a decision?"

"I have," she said. "I quit my job this morning. My bags are packed and I'm here to stay."

The news was an enormous weight off his mind. Things were now under control. She and the baby were finally safe.

"I should probably warn you that my car committed suicide about a hundred feet down the driveway."

"My condolences."

She shrugged. "The carburetor was terminally ill. I don't suppose you could spring for a new one. I'll reimburse you."

"I'll take care of it."

He might have worried it was just another scam, but he'd learned an awful lot about Tess these past few days. Since one could never be too careful in a situation like this, he'd hired a private detective to check her out. He'd found nothing in her past to indicate foul play. She had no criminal record, no past deviant or questionable activity. Nothing to suggest she might be conning him. Tess was exactly who she appeared to be. A hardworking woman just doing her best to get by. She had never wanted more from him than a little financial help.

With that knowledge, something deep in his soul felt oddly settled.

Not that he expected this to be easy. Making love with Tess had made him feel alive for the first time in months—had given him hope that he had a chance for happiness again. But even if he'd asked her to stay that night, if he'd let himself fall for her, a child would have never been part of the deal. Seeing Tess's growing belly would be a constant reminder of everything he'd lost.

He'd loved Jeanette, but she was gone. He'd accepted that. It was losing his son that still stung like a fresh wound. A slash through his heart that would never stop bleeding.

In some ways he felt ready to move on, in others he was still trapped in the past.

"So," Tess asked, dropping into the chair across from his desk, "how exactly is this going to work?"

"It will be exactly as we discussed the other day. You'll stay here with me until it's born. Afterward I'll set you and the baby up in a condo with a generous trust."

She gazed intently at him, as if she were trying to see into his head, to be sure what he said was true.

The color of her sweater seemed to draw out the yellow in her irises. He remembered thinking that night in the bar how unusual they were. How bright and full of curiosity, and maybe a little sad.

He'd watched her for a while before approaching her, fascinated by her petite, striking features. By her warm, genuine smile as she chatted with the bartender. And when she looked his way, and their eyes met and locked, there had been enough sparks to melt the snow on the entire mountain. It hit him with such force that it had nearly knocked him out of his chair.

Even now there was something about the woman that messed with his head.

"Sounds almost too good to be true," she said.

"Meaning...?"

"Look, it's not that I don't trust you, but..."

"But you *don't* trust me," he said, and she gave him a sheepish shrug. "I'm not offended. Put in your position, I wouldn't trust me, either."

"Honestly, you seem like an okay guy. A little overbearing maybe... It's just that I'm giving up an awful lot here. I'm watching my back, you know? I don't really know anything about you."

He understood completely. He would never enter into a business agreement on a handshake deal. "I've already spoken to my attorney about drawing up a contract."

She narrowed her eyes at him. "And I'm supposed to trust this attorney?"

"You're free to have the attorney of your choice look over the documents before you sign anything— at my expense of course."

"I guess that sounds fair."

"I should warn you that my lawyer has insisted on a confidentiality clause."

"*Confidentiality?* Who am I going to tell?"

"This is as much for yours and the baby's protection as mine. It was abhorrent the way the media exploited my wife's death. For months after, they made my life a living hell. There was an unauthorized biography written about her life and a made-for-television movie. Neither was what you could consider flattering, or had barely an ounce of truth. Trust me when I say that you don't ever want to know what that's like."

"When I found out from the girls at work who you were, I went to the library and did a little research."

"What kind of research?"

"Old newspaper articles and magazines, Internet stuff."

He wanted to feel indignant, but really he had done the same thing. "And what did you find?"

"There was a lot. So I get why you're worried."

"Things have finally died down. I don't want to stir the pot. The fewer people who know about this the better."

"I understand. I don't want that, either."

He didn't want to alarm her, but it was only fair that he caution her about what she might be getting herself into. "I'm not suggesting you should break all ties and avoid your friends—"

"I don't have any friends." She smiled and added. "I didn't mean that the way it sounded. Like, oh poor me I have no friends. It's just that I haven't lived here long and I work so many hours I never really found the time to make too many friends. Not close ones, anyway."

And now he was basically telling her not to make friends at all.

"Don't worry," she said. "I'll be careful."

"Then I guess that just about covers it," he said.

"Um, actually, there are a couple more things."

"Okay."

"I'm not sure how to say this, so I'm just going to say it. I won't live with an alcoholic. You have to stop drinking."

Her words took him aback. What had given her the impression he had a problem with alcohol? Because he had an occasional drink? Who didn't? Or had she read about him in the tabloids? Removing himself from the public eye, hiding away, had only served to fuel the media's interest. God only knows what rumors they had been spreading lately. He'd stopped paying attention a long time ago.

He opened his mouth to deny the accusation, then realized that was exactly what an alcoholic would do. Damned if he did, damned if he didn't.

Instead he asked, "If I refuse?"

"The deal is off."

Seeing as how he wasn't an alcoholic, it was a small sacrifice to make.

"I'll quit drinking," he told her.

She gave him a wary look, her pixie features sharpening with suspicion. "You'll quit drinking. Just like that?"

"Just like that." He walked over to the minibar, picked up the decanter of scotch he kept there and poured its contents into the sink. He enjoyed an occasional drink, but it wasn't something he couldn't live without.

She narrowed her eyes, as though she wasn't sure she could trust him. "You'll put it in the contract?"

"Done. Anything else?"

"After the baby is born, I'd like you to loan me the money to go back to school. I got my GED last year and I really want to go to college."

"I'll set up a trust that will ensure you'll never have to work another day in your life."

"Sitting around eating bonbons and getting facials may appeal to the women in your inner circle, but I want to do something with my life. I want to be able to look back and feel that I've accomplished something."

"I have nothing against working mothers. But I do believe a child should be raised by its parents, not a nanny or a babysitter."

Tess wondered if his movie star wife had been planning to give up her career once their child had been born.

Somehow she doubted it.

If Ben wanted to take care of his child financially, that was one thing. She was more than capable of taking care of herself.

"If it makes you feel any better," she said, "I agree completely with your values. I wouldn't even consider going back to work until the baby is in school. So it might take time for me to pay you back."

"I don't want you to pay me back."

"But I will anyway."

He looked as though he might argue, then gave his head a shake, like he realized it was probably useless. "Is there anything else?"

"The other day you said I could keep my doctor."

"If that's what you want."

"Good. Then, I guess that covers it."

One of those cute smiles curled his mouth and like a silly school girl she felt her knees go weak. The man was too good looking for his own good. He was wearing black again, as he had every single time she'd seen him—a good indication that he really didn't own anything that wasn't black. Maybe it was his trademark. She wondered if he wore black boxers, too. Or maybe bikinis.

Whatever his underwear preference, it was clear she'd made him happy, and for some reason that made her feel really good. The man had been through an awful lot. She'd tried to convince herself he was just some guy who happened to be the father of her baby. But when they were near each other she felt so...*aware* of him. Connected in a way that she didn't think had anything to do with the child she was carrying.

Even worse, she was pretty sure he felt it, too.

"I'll call my attorney and have him draw up the papers. Mrs. Smith will see you to your suite."

"Before you do, there's something about this that just doesn't make sense to me."

"What's that?"

"If you don't want the baby, why are you doing this?"

He was quiet for a moment and when he looked at her, his eyes were so sad. "I take responsibility for my actions."

She shook her head. "I don't think that's it. If you didn't care about this baby, it would have been a hell of a lot easier to pay me off and send me on my way."

"I never said I didn't care."

If he did care, why couldn't he be a part of the baby's life?

And just like that, something clicked. Suddenly this whole thing made sense. Why he insisted she stay here. Honestly, she didn't know why she hadn't figured it out before.

He blamed himself for his son's death. By keeping her here, he thought he was keeping her and the baby safe.

"Nothing is going to happen to me or the baby," she said. "I'm used to taking care of myself."

He gave her a look so full of pain and anguish she felt it straight through to her heart. "I didn't protect my son and now he's gone. That's one mistake I won't be making again."

The malevolent Mrs. Smith led Tess up the wide marble staircase to her room. Tess followed her through the ornately carved double doors—didn't they have any *normal* doors in this place—to what would be home for the next five months.

Her first impression was the sheer size of the room, but it mostly just looked dark and depressing. The scent of paint and new carpet lingered underneath the refreshing lilt of potpourri. She looked around for a light switch. "Don't you people ever turn on lights?"

Casting her a dour look, Mrs. Smith marched across the room and yanked open the heavy drapes shading the windows, flooding the room with warm afternoon sunshine. The transformation of dark to light made Tess gasp.

Decorated in warm beiges and soft greens, the room blossomed around her like a budding spring garden. The overstuffed furniture looked comfortable and inviting. The kind you could sink deeply into, curl up with a good book and lose yourself for an entire afternoon. She kicked off her shoes and dug her toes into carpeting so thick and luxuriant it felt like walking on pillows.

It was fresh and warm and alive. The perfect place to nurture the new life growing inside her.

If she had all the rooms in the world to choose, this would be the one she would pick.

"It's beautiful," she said. "And everything looks so new."

"And let's try to keep it that way," Mrs. Smith

said in that holier-than-thou tone. "Benjamin asked me to furnish you with whatever you need."

Orders she would follow, but not happily. But Tess was determined to remain marginally polite. She had the sneaking suspicion she would be running into this woman an awful lot over the next five months. Meaning that if she were so inclined, she could make Tess's life a living hell. "Thank you."

"I've taken the liberty of removing anything of value." She flashed Tess that condescending, distasteful look. As if Tess were not a houseguest, but something she'd scraped from the bottom of her shoe. Ben obviously hadn't instructed her to be nice.

Tess wouldn't give the old bird the satisfaction of knowing she'd bruised her pride. "Aw darn, my fence will be so disappointed."

With the ferocity of a mother bear protecting her cubs, she all but growled at Tess, "After all that Benjamin has been through, he doesn't deserve this. I won't let you hurt him."

Tess didn't point out that it took two to tango, and if Ben didn't want to be in this situation, maybe he should have become a monk. At the very least he shouldn't have taken Tess up to his room.

But what good would it do to try to defend herself when she was sure the frigid woman believed Tess had gotten pregnant on purpose? And Tess couldn't deny her own background. There was no escaping her social status. She'd been the last born in a long line of uneducated blue-collar workers. She hadn't even gone to college.

At least with her child Tess would be breaking the cycle.

"Dinner is at seven in the dining room," Mrs. Smith said in that cold, annoyed tone, then she turned and left, shutting the door behind her.

Tess let out a long, tired sigh and looked around, deciding the sooner she got herself settled in, the better. But she didn't see her bags. Across the room, through a second set of doors—ornate and gaudy of course—Tess found herself in an enormous bedroom. Not surprised that it was dark, she crossed the room and flung open the curtains, letting in a wash of golden sunshine. To her delight, the bedroom had been decorated in the same warm, earthy tones. She opened a set of French doors and stepped out onto the balcony, filling her lungs with fresh air. The view of the gardens below was breathtaking. Spring flowers exploded with color and rolling green grass seemed to stretch for miles. The white tips of the Scott Bar Mountains towered in the distance underneath a clear blue sky.

Wow.

This she could definitely live with.

She stepped back inside and found her bags waiting for her by the king-sized bed. She carried them to the cavernous walk-in closet, set them down then continued on into an enormous bathroom decorated in soft yellows with a Jacuzzi tub big enough for a family of four and an enclosed glass shower stall with two heads.

So this was how the other half lived. It was even more impressive than the presidential suite at the resort.

She rubbed her aching back and gazed longingly at the tub, then at her bags. Unpack first, bath later. But by the time she'd emptied her duffels and hung up all her things, she wanted nothing more than to lie down and rest.

Just a quick nap, she decided, then she would go exploring.

She stripped down to her birthday suit and pulled back the fluffy leaf patterned comforter and slipped beneath the cool, silky-soft vanilla-white sheets. She felt herself sinking as the mattress conformed to her body.

It was like curling up in a bowl of whipped cream. Within minutes she was sound asleep.

Ben pushed aside the drapes covering his office window and stood in a column of bright light, gazing out across acres of pristine rolling green grass and gardens blooming with vibrant shades of deep orange, sunny yellow and royal purple.

Jeanette would have loved this. It was exactly what she had envisioned when they bought this house. If he closed his eyes, he could imagine her out there, playing with their son. He would have been nearly a year old now. Maybe even walking. Saying his first words. In his imagination his little boy always had

Ben's dark hair and his mother's pale blue eyes and bright smile. He was always happy and laughing.

The door opened and he turned to see Mrs. Smith standing there, saving him from a landslide of painful memories. He let the curtain drop.

"Your guest is all settled in," she said.

"Thank you."

"Is there anything else?"

"No, nothing—oh wait, yes there is. I need you to go through the house and get rid of anything alcoholic."

She frowned. "Whatever for?"

"A condition of her staying here was that I stop drinking. She thinks I'm an alcoholic."

"And you let her believe—"

"It doesn't matter what she believes, I want her to feel comfortable here. Just do it please."

Mrs. Smith didn't look happy, but she didn't argue. "I'm going to say, again, that I don't like this arrangement."

"I know you don't." She hadn't liked Jeanette, either, but they had learned to coexist. She was so protective of him, the truth was, she would never think anyone was good enough.

"I know you still feel guilty, Ben, but it wasn't your fault."

He didn't have to ask what she meant. She had never said it to his face, but he knew she blamed his wife for his son's death. She'd always considered Jeanette spoiled and self-centered.

Her career had just been taking off when she found out she was pregnant. She'd been more annoyed than excited at the prospect of becoming a parent, by the physical limitations of her pregnancy. Afraid it would affect her career negatively—God forbid she get a stretch mark or two—she'd even talked briefly about terminating, but thankfully he'd managed to talk her out of it. He had been sure that given time to adjust, she would have enjoyed motherhood. At least, that had been his hope.

In the end, none of it had mattered.

"Have you called your parents?" Mrs. Smith asked.

His parents.

Having to explain this to his family was another problem altogether. They had never been overbearing or judgmental—quite the opposite in fact. He hadn't seen or heard from either of them since last Thanksgiving. That didn't mean it wouldn't be difficult for them to understand. In so many ways, they barely knew him. "Not yet."

"Don't you think you should?"

"Why? There's no point in getting them excited about a grandchild they're never going to see."

Four

Ben knocked on the door to Tess's suite, curious as to why she hadn't shown up for dinner. Why, in the three and a half hours since she'd arrived, she hadn't even ventured out of her suite.

No. He wasn't curious. He was downright worried.

According to Mrs. Smith she'd only had two bags and a couple of small boxes, so it couldn't have possibly taken her all this time to unpack. What if something was wrong? What if she was sick?

He knocked again, harder this time. "Tess, are you there?"

Knowing he probably shouldn't, he eased the door open. The sitting room was flooded with pinkish light from the setting sun. He'd always been fond of the color scheme, and Tess staying there seemed oddly appropriate somehow. Much like her, it was refreshing and cheerful and almost whimsical in its simplicity. And homey. That was what being with Tess had felt like.

Like coming home.

He stepped past the doorway and listened for the sound of movement. The suite was dead silent.

"Tess," he called, expecting an exasperated reply. In fact, if it meant she was all right, he welcomed a little sarcasm, but she didn't answer.

Fear looped like a noose around his neck, making it difficult to breathe.

What if she'd slipped and fallen?

What if she was hurt?

Without considering the consequences, he charged across the room to the partially open bedroom door and shoved his way through, his heart thumping against his rib cage. More muted sunshine and soft color—but no Tess. He stormed through her closet to the bathroom.

Empty.

Where had she gone? Had she snuck out? Had agreeing to stay here only been some sick joke to humor him?

He returned to the bedroom, teetering on the narrow ledge between anger and panic, when he heard a muffled snore from the vicinity of the bed. Only then did he notice the slight lump resting beneath a mountain of fluffy blankets.

Relief hit him so deep and swift his knees nearly buckled.

He'd been picturing her sprawled on the floor bleeding to death, and in reality she was only taking a nap.

He raked his hair back and shook his head. He had to get a grip, or this was going to be the longest five months of his life. He had to stop expecting the worst. She was safe here. The baby was safe. If he wasn't careful, he was going to drive her away. She wasn't his prisoner. She was a guest.

He considered waking her to see if she wanted something to eat, but decided against it. Though he hated the idea of her missing a meal, she obviously needed her sleep just as badly.

He walked over to the French doors and slid the drapes closed so the light wouldn't disturb her. Though his good sense told him to leave before she woke up and saw him there, he felt drawn to the bed. Drawn to her.

He couldn't screw this up. It was almost as if someone was giving him a second shot at this. The chance to keep this child and Tess safe. It wasn't a responsibility he planned to take lightly.

One quick look, he promised, just to be sure that she was all right, even though the steady cadence of soft breathing should have been assurance enough.

One quick look and he would leave.

The thick carpeting cushioned his steps as he crossed the room to the bed. Underneath an overstuffed comforter patterned with pale green leaves and yellow rose blooms, she lay curled on her side. She looked so small in the oversized bed, so vulnerable, like a nymph in a forest. Sweat beaded her forehead and dampened her upper lip and wisps of pale hair stuck to her cheek.

Would she overheat and make herself sick? It did feel awfully warm in here.

He very gently eased back the heavy comforter. Tess whimpered in her sleep and rolled onto her back. Only then, with the Egyptian cotton sheet clinging to her damp skin, exposing every dip and curve of her body in stark detail, did Ben realize she was naked.

Desire, swift and intense, rocked through him like a shock wave.

Get out now. And for God's sake don't touch her.

But she looked so pale against the cream-colored sheets. What if she wasn't just overheated? What if she was ill and burning up with a fever?

"Tess," he said softly, not wanting to startle her. She mumbled something incoherent and thrashed her head to one side. "Tess, wake up."

Don't do it, he warned himself, don't you dare touch her.

But the part of his brain that controlled his right arm apparently wasn't listening just then. He reached out and pressed the back of his wrist to her forehead, just as Mrs. Smith had when he was sick as a child, unsure of what it was exactly that he was supposed to feel.

Her skin was clammy and cool, which he took to be a good thing.

When he should have pulled away, he couldn't stop his hand from wandering over her skin, his fingers grazing the softness of her cheek. He liked her this way—all delicate and sweet and vulnerable. Her mouth looked soft and kissable. That night in the hotel he'd been addicted to her kisses. He'd been like an addict needing a fix, and when he woke the next morning to find her gone he'd craved her presence.

Even now, after all that had happened, there was something about Tess that he found irresistible.

Considering the position he held in Hollywood, not to mention coming from a wealthy family, he'd met his share of women with less than pure intentions. With Tess it had been different. As much as he hated the term, so *real*.

He wanted to feel that again. Which seemed unlikely now, given the circumstances. Or at the very least, not very smart. Even if these feelings he was having were mutual, she was having a child he could never accept. Definitely not the ingredients for a lasting relationship. Which is what she and the baby deserved. Someone to love them *both*.

Which would cause a person to wonder why he was still touching her.

He watched his thumb slip over the lush fullness of her lower lip, saw her lips part slightly and felt a puff of warm breath escape. The heat crawled up his thumb and into his hand, gaining momentum as it traveled through his arm and into his chest, kicking his pulse up a notch. He'd be damned if the woman didn't have a way of getting under his skin, making him feel.

From there the heat worked its way down in a swirl of sensation to his abdomen and settled firmly in the region just below his belt. The idea of bending down to brush his lips against hers, to feel that physical and emotional connection, was almost irresistible.

Almost.

Tess's eyes fluttered open and he jerked his hand away. She gazed up at him and her mouth curled into a drowsy, confused smile. "Hi."

Damn—she was pretty.

"Hi."

She looked around, puzzled by her surroundings, as if she'd forgot where she was. "You're in my room?"

She didn't sound angry, though she had every right to be. And he couldn't resist brushing the damp hair back from her forehead. What was it about her that made it so difficult to keep his hands to himself? "You didn't show up for dinner and I was worried. When I knocked and you didn't answer, I thought maybe something had happened to you."

Her eyes were still foggy from sleep and far too trusting. "Like what?"

Good question. It was obvious now that he'd over-reacted. "I don't know. I guess I just needed to know that you were okay. I should never have come in un-invited. I'm sorry."

No, he shouldn't have, but Tess couldn't work up

the will to be angry with him. She kept seeing the anguished look on his face when he talked about losing his son. Why didn't he just tell her how he really felt? Tell her he was scared?

Because he was a man, she reminded herself. And in her experience men didn't talk about their feelings. They never admitted fear. Especially men like him. They thought it made them weak.

Nothing about Ben Adams could be mistaken for weak. He was a walking powerhouse of pure testosterone and male perfection.

"I'm okay," she told him. "Just tired. It's been a long couple of days."

He stroked the hair back behind her ear. Despite how inappropriate his being here probably was, Tess didn't stop him. It was such a sweet gesture, and felt so good. Instead of telling him to leave, as she really should have, Tess closed her eyes and sighed.

After all, it's not as if he had never seen her in bed before. In bed *and* naked.

"That's nice," she said. "You did the same thing that night in the hotel."

"Did I?" He continued the gentle stroking, brushing past the shell of her ear, grazing her neck softly. Until it began to feel more than just *nice.* Exactly as it had that night. And for the same reason as then, she didn't reach up and wrap her arms around his neck, pull him down for a kiss. No matter how much she wanted to.

"You thought I was asleep. But I was only pretending."

"Why?"

She shrugged. "Maybe I was afraid that if I opened my eyes, you would tell me to leave. And maybe I wasn't ready to go."

"Why did you?" He stopped stroking and she looked up at him. His eyes were almost…sad. "Why did you leave?"

"What reason did I have to stay?"

"You tell me," he said. It was almost as if he wanted her to say she'd fallen for him. But at this point, what difference did it make?

"You can't deny we're both better off. Suppose I had stayed. Supposed we had fallen in love. And a month or so later I sprang the news on you that I was pregnant. Would you have been happy? Would it have made you want the baby any more than you do now?"

She could see by the look in his eyes and in the words that he didn't say, the answer to that question was no. It wouldn't have made any difference.

"It's not that I don't want it. I just…I can't do it." There was so much grief in his eyes, so much unresolved conflict. If he was ever going to get on with his life, he needed to learn to forgive himself.

She rolled on her side and propped herself up on her elbow, tucking the sheet under her arms. "Bad things happen to good people, Ben. Things we have no control over. It's no one's fault."

"And what about the things we do have control over? Who do we blame for that?"

She hated to see him sad and hurting when she

knew there wasn't a thing she could do or say to make him feel better. Only time would heal his wounds. The question was, how much time?

A year? Or ten? Or would he carry his guilt to the grave?

"Are you hungry?" he asked. "I could have something warmed for you."

Looked like their heart-to-heart was over. Would it always be this way? Every time she started to get close, would he push her away?

She rested her head back into the pillow. "I think I'd rather just sleep."

He nodded and rose to his feet. "I'll have a plate set aside in the fridge for you, just in case you change your mind."

"Thanks."

"Come find me tomorrow morning and I'll give you a tour of the house. I'm usually in my office."

"Okay."

"Good night, Tess. Sleep well."

"Good night."

He paused, looking as if he might say something else, then he turned and left. A second later she heard the door to her suite close.

She lay awake for a long time, watching the last traces of light disappear, counting the reasons why staying here was a good idea, so she could forget the reasons it wasn't.

The only thing she knew for certain is that she had to be careful. If Ben kept touching her so tenderly and looking at her with those lazy bedroom eyes she *was* going to do something stupid, like sleep with him. Then she would wind up doing something even *more* stupid.

Like fall in love.

Tess lay awake the following morning, not quite ready to roll out of bed. She'd slept over fifteen hours. Fifteen of the most restful hours she'd had in ages.

Despite everything, she felt comfortable here. And though yesterday she might not have been one hundred percent sure, she knew now that she was doing the right thing staying here. The right thing for her and the baby.

Knowing she no longer had to kill herself working too many hours, struggling to pay bills she couldn't afford, an enormous weight had been lifted from her shoulders. She felt a sense of peace she hadn't experienced in a long time.

The future was still blurry, but now at least she felt as if she were moving in the right direction.

She folded a hand over the little bump where her baby was growing. She couldn't wait to feel it move for the first time, and she was actually looking forward to getting big, even if that meant getting stretch marks. Since this first pregnancy could very well be her last, she wouldn't take a second of it for granted.

She only wished she had someone to share it with.

Some day soon she would have to think about getting maternity clothes. Though, without an income, she wasn't sure how she planned to pay for them. Her last check hadn't added up to much, and her savings were nearly depleted.

Maybe if she shopped at The Salvation Army. In the past she'd found some really awesome deals there. Designer labels—gently used—for dirt cheap. A girl did what she could to get by. No one could accuse her of not being resourceful.

And of course she could ask Ben to lend her money for clothes. She didn't doubt for a second that he would fall all over himself to accommodate her. In her experience, guilt could do that to a man. And if she were a different kind of woman she might take advantage of that. Lucky for him she had a conscience.

But Ben had done so much already. God only knows how she would ever pay him back.

She heard the door in the sitting room open.

Who could that be? Was it Ben coming to fetch her for the house tour. Or maybe he was coming to check on her, to see if she was still breathing.

She sat up, tucking the sheet close to her bare torso. Less than a minute passed before she heard the door close again. Whoever it was hadn't stayed long. Then the scent of bacon wafted her way. Her stomach rumbled and her mouth watered and she had to swallow to keep from drooling on herself.

She crawled out of bed, slipped her robe on and followed the scent to the table in the sitting room.

Someone had either anticipated her being ravenously hungry this morning, or they weren't sure what she liked.

There was a plate covered with three different types of eggs—omelet, scrambled and poached—and another piled high with pancakes, a delectable looking croissant and two slices of French toast. Beside that was yet another plate with sausage and bacon *and* a thick slab of ham. To drink she had a choice of orange juice, grapefruit juice, cranberry cocktail or hot tea.

Wow. Someone went all out. And because she hated seeing good food go to waste, she was sure she would eat way more than she should. She would have to ask Ben or the cook or whoever to take it easy on her portions or she was going to wind up gaining one hundred pounds.

With a body like hers, eight pounds of baby would be pushing the capacity.

On the table beside the tray lay a large white envelope with her name scrawled across the front. She picked it up and grazed her fingers over the letters, wondering if Ben had written it. She had no idea what his writing looked like. It was odd to be having a child with a man she knew virtually nothing about. To be living in his house.

She bit off a piece of bacon, grabbed the envelope and ripped it open. Inside she found a set of keys that did not belong to her car and a shiny new Visa card with her name on it.

The attached note read:

For whatever you and the baby need.

It was signed simply, B.

Wow.

She should have figured he would do something like this, yet every gesture of generosity still shocked her a little. He had an uncanny way of anticipating her every need. Not that she could accept this. But the polite thing to do would be to thank him. If her mother had taught her nothing else, she'd instilled Tess with good manners.

She quickly finished her breakfast, showered and dressed and headed down the stairs to Ben's office. She rapped on the door several times, but he didn't answer. Would it be okay to open the door and enter uninvited?

He'd come into her bedroom uninvited. Of course, that had been because he thought she might be maimed. Or dead. Besides, this was his office, not his bedroom. And he had told her to come get him this morning for a tour of the house.

So going in was probably just fine.

She reached for the knob…

"What are you doing?"

Tess jumped so high she nearly fell out of her shoes. She spun around and found Mrs. Smith standing there.

"You scared me," Tess said, her pulse pounding.

Mrs. Smith leered down her hook nose. "Why are you snooping around Benjamin's office?"

The old bat had an uncanny way of making Tess

feel like a deviant and she hadn't even done anything wrong. "I wasn't snooping. I was looking for him."

"He's not in his office."

Tess smothered an impatient sigh. "Where could I find him, then?"

"He's asked not to be disturbed."

It occurred to her just then that Mrs. Smith could be covering for him, hiding the fact that he was still drinking. Maybe he'd only said he would quit to get Tess to agree to stay.

Almost as quickly as the thought formed, she knew it wasn't true. Wouldn't she have smelled it on him last night when he came to her room? Wouldn't she have been able to tell by his behavior? She could spot a drunk a mile away.

Ben wouldn't have told her to come down to see him if he didn't mean it. No, there was only one person who didn't want Tess to see Ben.

Mrs. Smith.

"Tough," she told the old bag. "He left me something and I need to talk to him."

"If this is about the car, it's in the garage. The dark blue Mercedes."

A Mercedes? She'd never driven an import. In fact, she'd never driven anything under twenty years old and on its last leg. "I don't know if I feel right using his car."

"It's not his car. He ordered it for you. It was delivered this morning."

"Delivered?" Tess asked.

"From the dealership."

"Dealership?"

She gave Tess an exasperated look, as if she were addressing an obtuse child—or the village idiot. "Is English a second language for you? Yes, a *dealership.* Where they sell *cars.* You do know what a car is?"

Yeah, and there was no way the man actually bought her one. "So what, it's like a rental until mine is fixed?"

"No, it's a lease."

"He *leased* me a Mercedes?" What about her car? He said he would replace the carburetor.

"Benjamin is a very generous man," she said, looking at Tess with barely masked disdain. "Too much, I think."

Tess couldn't disagree with her. Generosity like Ben's was completely foreign to her. And unsettling.

"You know, I didn't ask for any of this," Tess told her.

"What you did or didn't ask for is of no consequence to me."

From the other side of the door Tess heard the phone ring. Only once, as if someone had answered it right away. Mrs. Smith's eyes widened a fraction and Tess knew instantly that she'd been lying about Ben not being in there. But when she made a move for the knob Mrs. Smith insinuated herself between Tess and the door.

She shot Tess a tight-lipped defiant look. "You're not going in there."

Five

"But Benji, I haven't seen you in so long!"

Ben sighed and shook his head. God how he hated that nickname. It was annoying when he was ten, downright embarrassing when he was a teenager, now he swore she did it just to piss him off. "I'm sorry, Mom, it's just not a good time for a visit."

Not for at least another five months. Why was it that he hadn't heard from his parents for months, and out of the blue his mom calls, determined to make the trip overseas to see him.

She always did have lousy timing. She had been on location filming for nearly every major event of his life. If she'd had the option of paying someone to give birth to him for her, she probably would have.

"I promise I won't get in the way. You won't even know I'm there."

"I have so much work I wouldn't be able to spend any time with you. In fact, I'll probably be going back to L.A. for a while." Big fat lie. He had no plans to leave the city. Or the house for that matter. "You know how much you hate it there."

He heard his mother sigh disappointedly and tried not to let it bother him. She hadn't been concerned with his feelings when she had to trot off and shoot a movie for eight weeks, or attend openings halfway around the globe. He didn't complain when his parents took their private vacations. Because they just *needed* to get away.

She had absolutely no right to expect anything from him. And still he felt guilty for telling her no.

From outside his office door he heard raised voices.

Aw hell, were Mrs. Smith and the cook going at it again?

"Mom, I have to let you go."

"But Benji—"

"Something's come up. I'll call you later. I promise." Much later. Like five months from now.

He hung up before she reduced herself to begging. He would have to stop answering the phone when she called.

He pushed himself up from his chair and crossed the room. He pulled the door open to find Mrs. Smith standing there with her back to him, arms spread as if she were guarding the doorway.

What the—?

Tess stood across the hall, cheeks bright with anger, fists clenched, looking ready for a fight.

A knock-down, drag-out brawl.

Mrs. Smith could be a mean old bird, but he'd put his money on Tess, hands down. She may have been little, but Tess has street smarts, and man was she tough.

"I told you that he doesn't want to be disturbed," Mrs. Smith snapped at Tess, in the scolding tone Ben recalled from his childhood. The tone that said she wasn't taking any crap.

"I don't care," Tess snapped back just as forcefully. "I need to talk to him."

Neither seemed to notice him standing there.

"Can't you just leave Benjamin alone?" she hissed. "Why is it that you insist on making this harder for him. He's giving that bastard child a decent life. Isn't that enough?"

Ouch.

Tess opened her mouth to reply, then noticed Ben standing there. Whatever she had been about to say evaporated, and by the look on her face he knew exactly what she was thinking. She was wondering if he'd heard that *bastard child* comment.

"What's going on here?" he asked.

Mrs. Smith let out an undignified gasp of surprise and swiveled to face him. The color leached from her already pasty face. "I—I told her before you don't like to be disturbed while you work, and I caught her sneaking in here."

"I wasn't *sneaking*," Tess said, giving Mrs. Smith the evil eye. And here he'd been under the impression Tess was afraid of his housekeeper. Most people were. Every now and then she even gave him the willies.

But if Tess had been, she'd apparently gotten over it.

"I asked Tess to come and see me today," Ben told Mrs. Smith. "I promised her a tour of the house."

Mrs. Smith forced a smile. "All you had to do was ask. I'd be happy to give her a tour."

He would bet his bank balance she'd be *happier* removing her own eye with a fork than spending time with Tess.

He leaned in the doorjamb and sighed. This was so not going to be fun. "Tess, could you excuse us please? Mrs. Smith and I need a quick word."

As his housekeeper moved silently past him into the room, Tess shot her a smug look. Ben had to fight a grin. It wouldn't have surprised him a bit to see her stick out her tongue.

Those two didn't realize just how alike they were. But to tell either would probably earn him a black eye.

"Give me five minutes," he told Tess. When he shut the door, she was smiling.

He turned to his housekeeper and could see by the starch in her spine she was going to make this difficult.

"Have a seat."

She looked down her nose at him—a real feat considering he was several inches taller than she was. "I'd rather stand."

"Please, Mildred."

She relented and sat primly on the edge of the seat opposite his desk.

"I know you won't like this, but I want you to stop interfering."

"I'm looking out for your best interests," she said, as if that justified her behavior.

"Be that as it may, I want it to stop. You don't even know her."

"Neither do you."

And it would seem Mrs. Smith wanted to keep it that way. "But I'd like to get to know her. Maybe I can't be a father to that *bastard child* she's carrying, but it's still mine."

She lowered her eyes to her lap.

"Have you forgotten that my parents weren't married when they had me?"

"It was said out of anger. I apologize for my thoughtlessness."

"Would you please drop the faithful employee martyr act?" He sat on the edge of his desk. "You're family, and I love you. I understand that you're only trying to protect me, but I want it to stop. Understand?"

She nodded.

"I know you still blame Jeanette for what happened."

She looked up at him. "Is that any worse than you blaming yourself?"

"And assigning blame hasn't gotten either of us anywhere. Has it?"

She shook her head.

"I know you didn't like Jeanette, and yes, she had her share of undesirable qualities. Who doesn't? Despite her faults, she was my wife and I loved her."

"And Tess?"

"What has she done to you to make you dislike her so? I think she's made it pretty clear that she wants nothing from me."

"She says that now."

"I know you don't like it, but as Tess reminded me, she didn't make this baby alone. I share equally in the responsibility."

"I still don't trust her."

"She may act tough, but I don't doubt for a minute that this is just as difficult for her as it is for me. If you take the time to get to know her, I think you might like her."

"And you?" she asked. "Do you like her?"

"I do like her." Probably too much for his own good. "So, do we understand each other?"

"Yes."

"You promise to stop meddling?"

She nodded.

"I want to hear you say it," he told her and she shot him an exasperated look. "Come on. Say, 'Ben, I promise not to meddle.'"

She rolled her eyes heavenward. "I promise not to meddle."

"See how easy that was?"

"May I go now?"

"Sure. Send Tess in on your way out."

He watched as she rose from the chair and walked to the door, and when she pulled it open, Tess all but fell into the room. Like perhaps she'd been leaning against it. Trying to hear their conversation maybe?

"Whoops!" she said, looking from Ben to Mrs. Smith. "I must have tripped."

Mrs. Smith shot him a look—one that asked, I'm supposed to be *nice* to her?—before she stepped past Tess and out the door. Ben folded his arms over his chest and grinned at Tess.

She shot him a look of pure innocence. "I wasn't listening, I swear. I was just…leaning."

"The door is sound proof," he said.

She made a *pfft* sound. "Which explains why I couldn't hear a darned thing."

He just shook his head.

"Oh, come on," she said. "Can you blame me? She hasn't exactly been nice to me."

"That shouldn't be an issue any longer."

"Yeah, sure," she said with a snort. "I'll believe that when I see it."

Man, did he like her. And he could see that having her around would, if nothing else, keep things interesting.

"How was your first night here? I take it you slept well."

"Like a baby."

"Did you enjoy your breakfast?"

"It was good. Although there was an awful lot of it."

"Sorry. I wasn't sure what you would like."

"That's what I figured. But I'm not picky. I'll eat pretty much everything. And in slightly smaller quantities next time, please."

"I'll let the cook know." He pushed off from his desk. "Are you ready for your tour?"

"I wanted to discuss something with you first." She stepped over to him. "I can't accept this."

She handed him the credit card he'd left in her room this morning.

"I got it for you," he said.

"And I appreciate the gesture. Really I do. I thought about it a lot and decided it's too much."

"No, it isn't, Tess."

"Yes. It really is. You're doing too much already."

"You can't tell me you don't need things. Just take it." He held out the card and she pushed his hand away.

"I have money, you know."

"Not that I enjoy playing *I can top that,* but I'm almost certain I have more. You and the baby are my responsibility now."

"The only person responsible for me, is *me.*"

What was he, a magnet for stubborn women?

She was so damned proud. It annoyed him almost as much as he admired her for it.

"And here," she said, handing him the car key. "I'd feel much more comfortable driving my own car."

Uh-oh. "That could be a problem."

She narrowed her eyes at him. *"Why?"*

"It's sort of…gone."

"Gone to be fixed?"

"Ah, no. Just gone."

"Gone where exactly?"

"Car heaven."

Now her eyes went wide. *"Car heaven?"*

He could see that she was losing her patience. Not that he could blame her. He wouldn't be real happy if someone had sent his car to the junkyard. Of course, his car wasn't a death trap on wheels. "I had a mechanic look at it. He said the car was worth half the cost of everything that needed to be fixed. Not to mention it was lacking most modern safety features. It wasn't safe."

"Ben, you said you would buy me a new carburetor."

"And I did. It's in the garage, in the Mercedes."

She closed her eyes and shook her head. "Cute."

"It was a sound investment, and it's a safe vehicle. Antilock brakes, air bags, GPS, the works."

"You sure you can even handle me operating a motor vehicle? What if I'm late? Suppose I'm out somewhere and I lose track of time. You may have an anxiety attack. Or call in the Marines."

"Nope. I have that covered." He leaned back and opened the top drawer of his desk, pulling out the phone he'd ordered for her. He held it up so she could see. "I'll just call you on this."

"Jeez! You bought me a phone, too? Is there anything else? A pony maybe?"

"Would you like a pony?"

She gave him that stern, squinty-eyed look. "You

would, wouldn't you? You would actually buy a pony just to spite me. You would probably build a stable, too. And hire a trainer, all because I dared you to."

Yeah, he probably would.

He just smiled. "Come on, Tess. You need a car, and I have an extra one. If you don't use it, no one will."

"What about Mrs. Smith? Can't she use it?"

"She has a Rolls."

"You bought your housekeeper a *Rolls-Royce?*"

He grinned. "Perk of the job. Now, will you drive it, or do I have buy that pony?"

She held out her hand. "Fine, I'll drive the car."

He dropped the key in her palm and handed her the phone. She stuck them both in the pocket of her jeans—jeans that were looking more than a little snug in the tummy. In fact, he was pretty sure she'd left the button undone.

"Now are you ready for the tour?" he asked.

"Let's do it."

She obviously needed new clothes and would eventually need things for the baby, but he wasn't going to push his luck with the credit card.

Not yet anyway.

After touring the house, Tess came to a conclusion.

Ben had *way* too much money.

Until she'd seen all the rooms, she'd never realized exactly how many of them there were. How freaking enormous the house really was. Four huge floors including the walkout basement.

Eight bedrooms, six full bathrooms and two half baths. Two full suites and servants' quarters. Two kitchens. A walk-in pantry stocked to the gills with enough canned and dry food to last an ice age.

He owned a library packed floor to ceiling with shelf after shelf of books. Biographies to classic literary fiction and everything in between. Hardback and paperback. And she was pleased to see that he even had a decent collection of romance and women's fiction—which he swore were sent to him by agents hoping to sell movie rights.

The lower level of the house was where he seemed to keep all his toys. There was a screening room scented of leather and new carpet with an attached projection room full of all kinds of funky electronic equipment that she assumed had something to with Ben's work as a producer. Next to the screening room he led her into a fully equipped exercise room that put most gyms to shame, which he told her she was free to use at any time day or night. The tour ended in a game room equipped with a dart board, a foosball and pool table and four full-size classic arcade games. There was also an attached kitchen and a full bar that was conspicuously devoid of alcohol.

Each room he led her into had been as dark and gray and depressing as the next. Until she hit a light switch or opened the drapes, revealing life and color and all of the subtleties and warmth that made a house a home.

And as interesting as the tour proved to be, Tess had been even more enthralled watching Ben as he led her from room to room. She found herself mesmerized by the casual yet confident way he carried himself. Sleeves rolled, hands dipped loosely in the pockets of his slacks. She'd never known a man who seemed so comfortable in his own skin. She was pretty sure he was oblivious to how gorgeous he was, or if he knew, he didn't care. Maybe that was part of what made him so attractive. She found herself hypnotized by the sound of his deep voice, drawn to his energy as he seemed to put his whole heart into everything he said and did.

Though they had yet to really connect on an intellectual level, she knew instinctively that she would be as attracted to his mind as to his killer body and handsome face. Despite his pampered upbringing and assumingly top-notch education, it was obvious Ben had never developed the over-inflated ego she would expect from a man in his position. As far as she could tell, he was generous and kind and an all-around nice guy—when he wasn't doing things to annoy her, that is.

She'd always had a tough time figuring men out. But despite his few slightly annoying habits—like stealing her car—being with Ben felt easier. More mature maybe. But in a way that had nothing to do with age or experience. She had dated *mature* men who psychologically never made it past their eighteenth birthday. The ones who say they're ready to take the relationship to the next level, then have kittens when they see the extra toothbrush on the bathroom sink.

Sharing space obviously wasn't a problem for Ben. In fact, she couldn't recall a single issue that he'd deemed a *problem*. He never seemed to complain about anything.

She didn't doubt that falling in love with him would be as natural and effortless as breathing.

Meaning she would have to work all the harder not to.

"So what do you think of my house?" he asked.

"It's nice," she told him. "Although, for some reason I wouldn't have pictured you in a house this big. I don't want to say it's pretentious. It's beautiful. It just doesn't seem to fit you."

"The big house was Jeanette's idea. She was a small-town girl with big dreams. I think that buying this house was her way of showing everyone back home that she'd made it. Despite the fact that I thought it was too big, I couldn't deny her that."

"I knew girls like that back in my hometown. Not that I can recall a single one accomplishing much though."

"Ironically, she never even spent the night here. The renovations weren't finished until after she died."

"Everything looks new."

"Most of it is. She worked with the decorator for months. She was so proud of it all."

She could see a lot of love in his eyes for his late

wife, but there was something else there. Regret maybe? Or was it just sadness?

"You must really miss her."

"Some things I miss, some I don't."

When she shot him a curious look, he simply said, "No marriage is perfect."

Was it possible that he and Jeanette didn't have a good marriage? Or that they'd been having problems?

She couldn't deny she was curious, but if he wanted her to know the intimate details of his relationship with Jeanette, he would tell her. She was in no position to go fishing.

"This isn't new." She ran a hand across the edge of the pool table, over the well-worn felt.

"I've had this since I was a kid." Ben followed her with those dark, inquisitive eyes, making her ultra-aware of every move she made. Aware of the way the soft felt tickled her fingers, how, depending on the mood, the move was almost enticing. Not that she'd meant it to be. At least, not consciously.

"You must play a lot."

"When I can't sleep, usually. It clears my head. Helps me sort things through. It's gotten a lot of use the past year. Do you play?"

"I'm more of a Ping-Pong girl. Not that I don't have fond memories of one pool table in particular."

"Really?" He gave her a look, one filled with playful curiosity, and she knew exactly what he was thinking. What every guy would think.

She couldn't resist smiling. "Get your mind out of

the gutter. It's nothing like that. It's where I had my first real kiss."

"Sounds romantic," he teased.

"It really was." She felt wistful just remembering. A girl never forgot the thrill of her first kiss. "It was a friend's older brother. I was fifteen and he was eighteen."

"An older man." Ben sat on the edge of the table, folding his arms across his chest, looking genuinely interested. "How did it happen?"

She sat beside him. It had been so long since she'd even thought about it, but she remembered every detail. "Well, my friend was upstairs helping her mom with dinner and I was in the basement with her brother Noah, watching him play pool. We were talking and somehow we got around to the subject of whether or not I had a boyfriend. When I told him no, he said he couldn't believe a pretty girl like me didn't have ten boyfriends. Then he asked if I'd ever kissed a boy. Of course I turned fifty shades of red."

"What did you tell him?"

"The truth. That I hadn't. Not really. Not a *real* kiss."

"So then what? He tossed you down on the table and planted one on you?"

She gave him a playful shove. "No. It was very sweet. He was sitting on the edge of the table, kind of like you are. I was standing in front of him." She pushed off the table and stood a couple feet in front of him. "Like this."

Ben unfolded his arms and rested his hands on the

table beside him, and for a minute he actually looked the way Noah had that day. They were both dark, and had that long-haired, simmering, rebellious look. And they were similar in personality. Very sweet when they wanted to be—with the potential to be thickheaded. Maybe that's why she was so attracted to Ben. He reminded her of her first crush.

"Then what happened?" he asked.

"He reached up and took one of my hands and kinda pulled me closer, so I was in between his legs."

"You mean like this?" Ben took her right hand in his and tugged her to him. Her heart fluttered wildly when her legs brushed against his inner thighs and all of the sudden they were this close.

"Uh-huh." Exactly like that. The memory of the awe and excitement and the rush of emotions came rolling back to her. She recalled the exact instant when she realized she was about to experience her first real kiss. She remembered exactly what his lips had felt like as they brushed across hers. How it was so slow and sweet, how he'd taken his time. The thrill of his lips parting and his tongue touching her. Some girls she knew still thought tongue kissing was gross, but Tess had just about melted. He tasted warm and exciting and forbidden. A blend of cigarettes, soda and lust.

At the time she didn't recognize what lust was exactly. She just knew it was a feeling she liked.

She still liked it.

Too much.

Ben's eyes searched her face. He was so close she could feel the warmth of his body through his clothes. She could feel the whisper of his breath on her lips when he asked, "Then what did he do?"

She knew that if she told Ben, he would kiss her. And then who knows what might happen? She wasn't a fifteen-year-old girl any longer with naiveté and fear still on her side to help stop things before they got out of control. She had needs and desires just like Ben and she didn't trust herself to put on the brakes.

As much as she wanted him to kiss her, she knew she couldn't let him do it.

"After a few heavy-duty make out sessions over the next couple of weeks, he got Tracy Fay Bejarski pregnant, got married in a shotgun wedding and moved into a single wide across town."

He took the hint and, with a trace of regret in his eyes, let go of her hand. Regret she could definitely identify with.

She took a step back.

"Not exactly a happy ending," he said.

"I was devastated. A couple of kisses and I thought it was true love. Things were pretty bad at home, and I used to fantasize we would fall in love and run away together. I should be grateful. He didn't make much of his life. He and Tracy Fay divorced after baby number four and last I heard he's working nights at the gas station and spends the better part of his days in the bar."

"Benjamin?"

They both turned to find Mrs. Smith in the doorway. Tess wondered how long she'd been standing there watching them. How much she'd heard.

"Lunch is ready," she said.

"We'll be right up," Ben told her.

Mrs. Smith shot them a slightly suspicious look, then turned and left.

"Actually, I think I'll skip it," Tess said. "I'm still pretty full from breakfast. I think I'll take a walk in the gardens instead."

"Are you sure?"

"Yeah. I think the fresh air will do me good." For some reason she felt as if she needed a little time alone. Time to clear the unpleasant memories.

And the pleasant ones.

"I'll have the cook put something aside for you, in case you change your mind."

"Thanks."

He turned to leave and made it as far as the door before he turned back. "You know, you're right. It was a good thing it didn't work out between you and your friend's brother. You deserve better."

Maybe he was right, but she'd learned the hard way that the less you expected from life, the less you were disappointed when you didn't get what you wanted.

Six

Ben sat at his computer hitting Delete to erase the dozen e-mails his mother had sent in the week since their last phone conversation, the day Tess had arrived. Why on earth was she suddenly so determined to insinuate herself into his life? Could her timing be any worse?

His office door swung open and he looked up to see Tess standing there.

"Back from your morning walk?" he asked.

She stormed over to his desk, wearing that squinty-eyed, furious look she'd had the other day when he informed her that he'd gotten rid of her car.

"What did you do with them?" she demanded,

hovering over his desk, looking as if she might lunge over and throttle him.

Well, someone's panties were in a twist. And damn, she was cute when she was angry. A compact package of attitude and sass.

"Do with what?"

"*My clothes*," she said through gritted teeth. "I came back from my walk to take a shower and they were all gone."

He had the almost overwhelming urge to pull her in his arms and kiss that scowl right of those pretty pink lips.

He was quite sure if he did, she would deck him.

"Are they?" He calmly folded his arms over his chest and leaned back in his chair. "Have you checked the laundry?"

She slammed her hands down on her hips. "Why would the clean clothes that were hanging in my closet this morning be in the dirty laundry? Even my underwear are missing!"

He shrugged. "It was just a thought. I could ask Mrs. Smith if she's seen them."

Her cheeks flushed red with anger. "Give them back."

"I can't give you back something I don't have." He pushed up from his chair and walked across the room to the fireplace. He grabbed the iron poker and jostled the embers smoldering there.

Her eyes went wide and her mouth fell open in horror. "You *didn't*."

He set the poker back in the rack and turned to her, a confused look on his face. "Didn't what?"

She marched over to where he stood, gazing into the fireplace then looked up at him, aghast. "You *burned* my clothes?"

She was beside herself with anger—and completely adorable. He tried to look sympathetic, but a smile was breaking through.

"Oh my God! You think this is *funny?*" She darted a glance around the room, as if she were searching for something to throw at him. Or bludgeon him with.

"You need clothes, Tess. Otherwise you wouldn't be wearing shirts that are too tight and jeans you can't even button."

"What are you, the fashion police?" She tugged her shirt down in an attempt to cover the waist of her jeans, but it was—as he'd suspected—too small. "Besides, that is *not* the point."

"You said you have money, right? So what's the problem? Just buy new clothes."

"Yes, I have money, but not for an entire wardrobe!"

"Well then, I have the perfect solution." He slipped the credit card from his back pocket. The one she'd refused to take five days ago. "You can use this."

"You are unbelievable. Is there *nothing* you won't do to get your way?"

"Use this and you can save your money for a time when you really need it."

She looked as if she might burst with frustration.

"Don't you get it? I don't feel comfortable taking anything else from you. I hate owing people money."

If they were going to get into a debate on who owed whom, he owed her and the baby a hell of a lot more that she would ever know. More than he would ever be capable of giving. "You're not taking anything. I'm offering."

She looked at him like he was nuts. "What's the difference?"

"Tess, do you have any clue how much money I have?"

"Yeah," she snapped. "Way *too* much."

"Please," he said. "Let me do this for you."

Something in his face must have revealed his feelings, because her expression softened from anger to mild annoyance.

"Fine," she said after a moment. "But I'm going to pay you back. I don't know when, and I don't know how, but I'll return every penny that I spend."

"If that's what you want." He didn't bother to tell her he would never accept money from her.

He would burn that bridge when they came to it.

He held out the card and she reluctantly took it. "Don't believe for a second that you're completely off the hook here. I'm still mad as hell at you. If you do anything even remotely close to as stupid as this ever again, it's going to be your clothes in the fireplace next time. And you'll be shopping for new clothes completely naked, because I'll get it all."

A grin tugged at the corner of his mouth. He

didn't doubt for a second that she would do it. "I'll keep that in mind."

She shook her head, grumbling under her breath as she turned to leave.

"Will I see you at dinner tonight?" he asked. Every night since she'd arrived they had shared dinner together. And lunch.

She looked back at him over her shoulder. "Maybe I'll see you, maybe I won't. It just depends on how mad I still am at you." Then she left, slamming the door shut behind her.

No, she would be there. Because as angry as she might have been, he had seen something else dwelling just below the surface.

Relief.

She knew damned well she needed things, but she didn't want to spend the last of her money. She was the kind of woman who liked to keep a little extra for a rainy day. It made her feel safe.

What she didn't seem to get, or just hadn't accepted, was that she never had to worry about money again. She would be taken care of for the rest of her life, no exceptions. He would see to that.

Once he made a promise he didn't break it.

"That was wonderful," Tess said, wiping away any last traces of chocolate mousse from the corners of her mouth. She settled a hand on her overstuffed stomach. "I ate way too much again."

Ben sat across from her, sipping a steaming cup of coffee. "I'll tell the cook you enjoyed it."

She leaned back in her chair and sighed with contentment. Though she'd considered being a no-show, she'd decided to have dinner with him despite his stunt this afternoon.

She'd confronted him earlier feeling as if she would never forgive him, never trust him again, then he'd smiled—an adorable grin filled with amusement and affection—and it had been nearly impossible to hold on to the anger. He'd just looked so happy that he'd gotten what he wanted, and while normally that would have annoyed her even more, she realized in his own clueless male way, he meant well. Despite what she might have believed when she moved here, Ben really wasn't trying to manipulate or control her. He just wanted to take care of her.

It was tough to fault a guy for being generous and kind, even if his methods were slightly off the wall. And she couldn't deny driving a fifty thousand dollar car and shopping her heart out had been a blast.

After a couple of hours in town shopping, she'd begun to feel a little like Julia Roberts in *Pretty Woman*. Except, of course, that she wasn't a hooker, and Edward hadn't gotten Vivian pregnant.

And this wasn't a movie. It was real life. Ben wouldn't be sweeping her off her feet, or in Vivian's case, off a fire escape. They wouldn't ride off into the sunset together in his limo and live happily ever after.

"So," Ben said, dropping his napkin on the table. "What would you like to do now?"

She shrugged. "I don't know. What do you want to do?"

Although she already had a pretty good idea. He'd been teaching her to play pool. Rather unsuccessfully.

"Game room?"

"Why, so you can slaughter me at pool?"

"We don't have to play pool." He had this grin, like he knew something she didn't. What was he up to now?

Honestly, she was afraid to ask.

"I told you, video games were never really my thing and I suck at foosball."

"So we'll do something else," he said.

"Darts?"

"Nope."

Now she was getting curious, which with him could be a dangerous thing. In more ways than one. Since their almost kiss on the pool table the other day, they had both been pretty good about keeping their hands to themselves. Ben's eyes were another matter altogether. It seemed he was always watching her, studying her. But not in a way that made her feel uncomfortable. Instead she felt so...*aware* of herself. Aware of him.

Even though she shouldn't be.

"You'll see," he said, rising from his chair, motioning her to join him.

"All right." She got up and followed him downstairs to the game room, all the while feeling he had something up his sleeve. She found out what it was when he switched on the game room light, and she saw the brand new Ping-Pong table sitting there.

She groaned and shook her head. "You can't go a week without spending money on me, can you?"

He shrugged apologetically. "Sorry. It was this or the pony, and we both know how you feel about that."

The man was hopeless. "You really do have too much money, don't you?"

He grinned and handed her a paddle. "Want to play?"

Of course she did. She took the paddle from him. "I have to warn you, I'm pretty good. I might bruise your ego."

"It's been bruised before," he said, taking one side of the table.

"That's what you think." She flashed him a devilish smile. "Ten bucks says I whup your behind."

Tess did whup him. Repeatedly and shamelessly. But Ben redeemed himself by decimating her at a game of pool.

If it had been Jeanette playing, she would have pouted and complained over losing. If she couldn't do something perfectly, she didn't like to do it at all. She'd been incredibly competitive.

Tess on the other hand didn't seem to care who won or lost, as long as they were having fun. And they did have fun. She had a playful, almost silly side that was unexpectedly refreshing. She brought light into a world that had been too dark far too long. She gave him hope.

Though, hope for what, he hadn't figured out yet.

After an hour of fierce competition, they took a break and Ben got them each a bottle of water from the refrigerator behind the bar.

"That was fun," she said. "I haven't played Ping-Pong in a long time."

"It was fun," he agreed.

"If I wasn't here, what would you be doing? What was a typical Friday night for you?"

He leaned on the bar and took a swig of his water. "Either work or watch television."

"I thought you Hollywood types did exciting things, like going to parties or night clubs."

"Not anymore. All Jeanette ever used to want to do was go out barhopping and it seemed as though there was always someone throwing a party we just *had* to be at."

"You didn't like that?"

"Occasionally I don't mind getting out. But the truth is, I'm more of a homebody."

Tess leaned forward and rested her elbows on the bar, propping her chin on the backs of her hands. "I'm exactly the same way. Give me a good movie, a bowl of popcorn and a comfy couch to curl into and I'm in heaven."

"You like movies, huh?"

"I *love* movies."

"What kind?"

"I'll watch pretty much anything. I'm a movie junkie. The employees at Blockbuster know me by name."

"Then there's something I should show you."

Her brow furrowed. "Uh-oh, you have that look. The one you get just before you give me stuff. What did you buy this time?"

He flashed her a grin. "I didn't buy you a thing. I promise."

He led her upstairs to the den where he kept all of his entertainment equipment. Besides his office, he spent most of his time here. It was the one room in the house he'd insisted on having input in as far as interior design went.

He motioned to the door that was nearly hidden in the seams of the rich wood paneling. "See that door?"

She squinted in the direction of the wall. "Oh, yeah. A hidden door. Cool."

"Open it."

"How? There's no knob."

"Give the right side a push and the door will pop open."

She gave him a look, like she wasn't sure she should trust him. "You promise there isn't a pony in there?"

"I promise."

She gave the door a push. The latch clicked and the door swung open and Tess gasped.

"Oh my God." She stared openmouthed at row after row of DVDs, floor to ceiling, spanning either side of the narrow four foot deep closet. "You must have every DVD in existence."

"Probably close to it," he said. "You like it?"

"*Like* it? It's amazing."

He watched with a smile as she stepped inside and ran her hand along a row of cases, as if she were soaking up their essence through the pores in her hand, a look of pure delight on her face.

"You could say I'm a movie junkie, too."

"I guess. Have you watched them all?"

"Most of them I've seen at one point or another. A lot of the older movies I haven't watched on DVD yet."

"I love old movies. John Wayne and Jimmy Stewart. And I love Hitchcock. *Psycho* is my all time favorite horror flick."

"Would you like to watch something?"

Her eyes lit up. "Could we?"

"Sure. Unless you're too tired." She typically retired to her suite before ten, and it was almost nine-thirty.

"I won't kill me to stay up late one night."

"Pick something. They're in alphabetical order, sorted by genre."

She spun in a slow circle. "I don't even know where to begin. On this shelf alone I see four or five possibilities."

"I have a lot of television series sets, too."

He watched as she scanned shelf after shelf of titles, still shaking her head in amazement. She looked so…happy. He liked that he could do this for her. That her stay here would be a pleasant one. She deserved it.

"How about this one," she asked, choosing an old Spencer Tracy-Katharine Hepburn film still sealed in plastic. "I haven't seen this in years."

"Sounds good to me." He took it from her and started setting up the system. "Go ahead and take a seat."

"Hey, Ben?"

He switched on the DVD player. "Yeah?"

"I just wanted to thank you."

He turned to her. She had a smile on her face. But her eyes looked sad.

"For putting on a movie?"

"For everything."

He was about to tell her there was no need to thank him. He owed her and the baby, and he would do anything to see that they both came out of this healthy and happy. But he didn't think that was what she needed to hear. She already knew that.

So he said the only thing he could say. "You're welcome."

It was after eleven when the movie ended. Not that Ben had spent a whole lot of time with his eyes on the screen. As always, he found that watching the woman stretched out on the couch across the room was a much more pleasing way to pass the time.

How was it that he never tired of looking at her? She wasn't the kind of woman who strutted into a room and stunned every man with her breathtaking beauty. She was much more subtle than that. So soft and petite, but sturdy somehow. Cute and sassy, and almost wholesome, until she opened her mouth and fired off a dose of attitude.

In the same way he had been attracted to Jeanette's fire and lust for life, Tess's quiet, determined nature fascinated him. He'd met more than his share of women over the years, through business or socially, but he couldn't recall ever knowing anyone quite like her.

When the credits began to roll on the screen, Tess turned to him and smiled. "That was *so* good."

Since he hadn't really been paying attention, he would take her word for it.

She yawned and stretched. "I wish we had time for another one, but I'm exhausted. I'm usually sound asleep by now."

He switched on the lamp beside his chair and used the remote to shut off the television. "We can do it again tomorrow night."

He walked over to the couch and held out a hand to give her boost up. She accepted and let him pull her to her feet. "I'll walk you to your room."

She yawned again and walked with him to the stairs. Mrs. Smith had already gone to bed and most of the lights were turned off.

"I'll probably sleep in tomorrow. Lately, if I don't get at least eight hours, I'm like the walking dead."

"Jeanette had that, too," he found himself saying. He didn't mind talking about Jeanette, but talking about her pregnancy was tough. Too many memories.

She smoothed a hand over her belly, a look of pure and complete contentment on her face. "It's worth it."

Another way she and Jeanette were so very different. Jeanette had flat out told him he had better be happy with one child, because she wasn't planning on doing the *pregnancy thing* ever again. Not that he thought it made her a bad person. She just had different priorities. Her career meant everything to her. She'd worked damned hard and sacrificed a hell of a lot to make a name for herself.

As much as he admired and appreciated his wife, he admired and appreciated Tess for all her differences.

"Does it kick yet?" he heard himself ask.

Where had that come from? He didn't want to know any more about the baby than necessary. All that mattered was that it was healthy.

"Not yet. Although I have felt flutters that may or may not be Braxton Hicks or indigestion. I'll ask next week at my five month checkup."

Five months already, meaning it had been nearly a month since she'd first come to give him the news. It seemed like only yesterday, so why did he feel as if he'd known her a lifetime? What was it about her that made him feel so…connected?

"I can leave a note for Mrs. Smith to have your breakfast brought up a bit later tomorrow morning if you'd like."

"That would be nice," she said. "As long as it's no trouble."

He didn't ask any more questions about the baby

and thankfully she didn't offer any details. When they reached her suite, they both stopped outside the door. Tess gazed up at him through the dim light, a sleepy, contented smile on her face. "I had a *really* good time tonight."

"I did, too."

She looked at the door, then back at him, her bottom lip clamped between her teeth.

"Anything wrong?" he asked.

"No. I just…" She lowered her eyes.

"You just what?" he asked, and the next thing he knew, Tess's arms were around him in a bone crushingly enthusiastic hug.

Seven

Aw, hell.

Ben steeled himself for the slam of emotion as her belly bumped his stomach. He waited for the grief to grab hold and drag him down. But instead of feeling pain or guilt or even aversion—and ah, man, he almost wished he had—desire snuck up and pounced on him like a wild animal, digging its claws and teeth into his flesh, sinking through skin and muscle straight to the bone.

Her scent suddenly seemed to be all around him. The same as before—sweet and sexy and enticing as hell—but different somehow. Maternal, maybe, if that made any sense. Or was even possible. Could a woman smell pregnant? And if she did, would it be so damned...*erotic?*

Her cheek settled against his chest, the softness of her hair snagging in the stubble on his chin as her hands settled on the flat of his back just below his shoulder blades. And damn did it feel nice. He'd forgotten how it felt to be close to her. The excitement and contentment. As if he were right where he was supposed to be. If it weren't for the baby...

He had intended on patting her back a couple of times, then backing away, but his arms were already around her. One hand curling over the base of her skull, his fingers tangling through her short silky blond locks. The other had made itself right at home dangerously low on her back. An inch lower and he'd be copping a feel of her sweet behind.

Holding her now, months later and after all they had been through, still felt the same, like...coming home. A place where everything was warm and sweet and familiar. He wanted to crawl inside the feeling and hold himself there.

He wanted to be inside of her.

And she would know just how much in another ten seconds, when the last of his blood left his brain and drained into his crotch.

Tess sighed, melting a little deeper into Ben's arms. Though she knew it was probably just an illusion, she felt so close to him.

When he'd asked about the baby kicking, it had been close to impossible to contain her excitement.

To stop herself from gushing out every little mundane detail about her pregnancy. She knew if anything spooked him, that would be it.

She closed her eyes and breathed in the scent of spicy cologne and male heat, felt bands of lean muscle flex under her hands. She rubbed her cheek against the silky fabric of his shirt, heard the steady thump of his heart. His long hair hung down and tickled her forehead, and suddenly every cell in her body ached to be touched. Her lips begged to be kissed. And *oh,* what the man could do with his mouth.

Bone-melting, toe-curling, out-of-this-world kisses. It was all coming back to her now. Not that she'd ever completely forgotten. She'd just blocked out a few crucial details. Like the way he'd been demanding yet achingly tender when he'd touched her. The way he'd given back twofold whatever he took. She'd never been with a man more interested in satisfying her needs than his own. In fact, she'd lost count of how many times he'd *satisfied* her.

The truth is, it had been so perfect, so amazingly wonderful, it had scared her half to death. After he'd fallen asleep, she had lain there wondering what she'd done. She knew nothing about him. She'd met him in a bar for goodness' sake. Her days of acting irresponsibly, of taking stupid chances and getting mixed up with the wrong kind of man, were supposed to be over. Moving to Prospect had meant turning over a new leaf.

Even if he hadn't been completely bad news—

which at the time seemed unlikely given her tendency to attract men who were nothing but trouble—he'd already said that he didn't want a relationship.

And like a fool, she'd ignored all her instincts and had gone and fallen in love with him.

"Tess," Ben said softly. He cupped her cheek and tipped her face up to meet his. It was dark in the hallway, but she could see the desire in his eyes as he gazed down at her. So fiery and hot she felt herself melting.

He was actually going to do it. He was going to kiss her. She knew it was wrong, but she'd been aching for it for so long now, it was almost a relief to finally get it over with. To get past that unresolved thing that always seemed to hover between them.

Ben's head began to tip and drift lower, his lips closer and closer, his hair tickling her cheek. He smelled so good, felt so solid and strong. She let her eyes flutter closed, let her head sink down into the cradle of his palm.

Oh, yes...

She felt hot all over and dizzy with anticipation, as if the hall were spinning around her. Ben dipped lower and lower, hovered there for a second, his breath warm and sweet on her lips.

"Tess," he whispered, and she held her breath, waited for that first brush of his lips, the hot taste of his mouth. He came closer, closer and her knees began to tremble...

And his lips softly brushed her cheek, just below her right eye.

"Good night, Tess."

Then he was gone, swallowed up by the darkness, and she was left standing alone in the hallway, too stunned to utter a sound.

Several minutes passed before she realized what had happened, before her hormone drenched brain cleared enough for the message to get through.

She didn't know if she should feel dejected or relieved or just plain thankful that at least he had had the good sense to put the brakes on.

Right now all she could feel was hopelessly confused. Did he want her or didn't he? Okay, dumb question. There was no denying he had been more than a touch turned on. She'd felt it. So why did he walk away?

Tess leaned against the suite door, still warm, weak and shaky.

She couldn't deny feeling as if she and Ben had reached some sort of turning point.

The question was, which way should they go?

Ben sat in his office working on his second cup of morning coffee and reading e-mail when something compelled him to get up from his seat and look out the window. His Tess-radar as he'd come to call it. Sure enough, when he eased back the curtain, there she was wandering through the garden. As she had every morning since she'd come to stay with him.

They shared meals, played Ping-Pong and pool and watched movies and television together. Other times they lost themselves in conversation, talking for hours. Sometimes late into the night. Despite coming from completely different backgrounds, they had a common bond. They understood each other.

In only a month's time she had become such an integral part of his life, he could hardly recall what it had been like without her there. The thought of her leaving, of things changing, was difficult to grasp, though he knew it was inevitable.

He let his forehead rest against the cool pane of glass. As she strolled slowly down the path, he allowed himself the privilege of watching her, of noticing all the changes in her body. She was beginning to look soft and round where she was once lean and angular. With the arrival of summer just weeks away, she'd been spending more time outside and her once pale, milky complexion was golden tan from hours in the sun.

Since that night outside her suite, they'd managed to keep their hands to themselves. No more almost-kisses, cheek or otherwise, and limited physical contact. It was as if they had established a silent understanding. An unwritten law that dictated just how far they would allow themselves to go.

At times he would go an entire day without an impure thought. Then she would smile at him a certain way or lightly touch his arm as she brushed past him and he would have to fight to keep from ravaging her on the spot.

And despite their best efforts to behave, there was

a feeling in the air, a tension growing between them and eventually something was going to have to give.

Though he almost never went outside, his feet carried him out of his office, through the house and out the back kitchen door to the path that led into the garden. When he reached Tess, she was kneeling down, her nose buried in a fuchsia bloom.

For a minute he just looked at her. She wore a pair of white capri pants and a gauzy blouse that looked almost transparent in the sunshine. She was humming to herself, slightly off-key. Some tune he didn't recognize.

"Good morning," he said.

Tess looked up at him, shielding her eyes from the sun, a bright smile lighting her face. "Good morning. You came outside."

She sounded so surprised, and pleased. Probably because she'd never seen him do it. He didn't know when the idea of leaving the house had become so unappealing. It wasn't even something that had happened gradually. He'd just stopped going out. The one and only exception had been that night at the resort, and look what had happened then. "Yep. I came outside."

She sat back on her heels. "Huh, and you didn't turn to ash."

"Ash?"

"As dark as you keep it in the house, when I first moved in, I honestly considered wearing garlic around my neck. Just in case."

He could feel a grin tugging at the corners of his mouth. He nodded to the blooms resting beside her where she knelt on the path. "Picking flowers?"

"I hope you don't mind. The gardener was giving me the evil eye earlier."

"Someone should enjoy them." He offered his hand and helped her to her feet. Her hand was small, warm and soft in his and he resisted the urge to keep holding it.

To keep his hands safely to himself, he slipped them into the pockets of his slacks.

"Will you walk with me?" she asked, and when he looked back toward the house she said, "Just for a few minutes."

When she gave him that sweet, hopeful look, how could he say no? "Just for a few."

They walked side by side down the winding cobblestone path bordered on either side by lush perennial gardens, chatting about the film he was considering working on. He closed his eyes and filled his lungs with clean mountain air scented with sweet fragrant blooms. The sun felt soothing and warm on his face and soaked into the black fabric of his shirt like hot molasses. "It's really beautiful, isn't it?"

She nodded, looking just as content as he was feeling. Linking arms, or resting an arm across her shoulder would the be the most natural thing in the world right now, but he didn't let himself go there. And the longer they spent this way, the harder it would be to resist.

"This is nice, isn't it?" she asked him. "Taking a walk, I mean."

"It is," he admitted. "But I am going to have to get back to my office. I'm expecting a call at eleven."

She held up the bunch of flowers she clutched in her hand and inhaled the sweet-smelling blooms. "You wouldn't happen to have a spare vase lying around that I could keep these in."

"You could probably get one from the kitchen. Ask the cook."

"The one who doesn't speak English?"

"Floero," he said. "That's vase in Spanish."

"I didn't know you speak Spanish."

"All my life we've had Hispanic employees. You pick up bits and pieces."

"What else can you say?"

"Sus ojos brillan más brillante que las estrellas." Your eyes shine brighter than the stars.

She laughed. "That's more than bits and pieces."

He grinned. "I might have taken a year or two of Spanish in school."

"Which was it? A year, or two?"

"Four, actually. It was an easy A."

"So, what did you just say?"

"I said, I have to get back to work." He didn't want to, but he did. For the first time in a long time he didn't want a reason to stay inside.

"Liar."

He feigned an innocent look, and touched his chest. "Who me?"

"I'm not sure exactly what you said, but I know it had something to with stars and eyes."

He shot her a questioning look.

She just smiled. "I speak a little Spanish, too."

A month earlier, if someone had told her she would be living in Ben's house, totally dependent on him and actually enjoying it, she'd have laughed herself silly. But here she was, having a good time. It was true that it would all come to an end, but then she would have the baby to take care of and focus on and she probably would be too busy to miss Ben.

At least she hoped that was the case.

"You know that I consider you a friend?"

"I do, too," he said. "I wish things could always be this way, but after the baby is born…"

What? They would suddenly not be friends anymore? She got it. And she could see that he was trying to figure out a way to explain it that wouldn't hurt her feelings.

"I'll be leaving," she said. "I'll have my condo and you'll have your mansion and we won't see each other."

"It's not you, Tess."

No, it was the baby, which was even worse. But she understood. At least, she was trying to. "It's okay, Ben, I get it."

But it wasn't okay. It hurt. And there wasn't a thing she could do to change it. To make it better.

He stood there for a second, just looking at her.

He reached up and brushed the hair back from her face and tucked it behind her ear. Then he turned and walked away.

Tess couldn't sleep.

She lay in bed that night until after midnight, long past when she usually fell asleep, working the situation between her and Ben over and over in her head.

After their conversation that morning, they had both gone on to act as if nothing had changed. Business as usual.

Only, something *had* changed.

She knew Ben didn't want the baby, or more to the point, wouldn't let himself want it, but to actually hear him come right out and say it again. It just felt so...final.

It was difficult to not resent him, to not take him by the shoulders, give him a rough shake and demand to know what was wrong with him. But she already knew what was wrong. And she felt so helpless because there was no way to fix it. Ben had to work this one through himself. Only when he was ready would he face his past and move on.

The question was, could she wait that long? Did she even want to try?

She was already in over her head. Already cared for Ben more than she should. More than was safe.

It was time to put a lock around her heart and swallow the key.

She rolled over and looked at the clock. Twelve-fifteen and she was still wide awake. On top of that, she was feeling the sting of heartburn creep up her esophagus. Maybe warm milk would do the trick. That was what her mom used to drink when she couldn't sleep.

She climbed out of bed, slipped on her robe, and headed downstairs. The house was dark and quiet and full of shadows this time of night. A little creepy in fact, but she didn't want to turn on a bunch of lights and wake anyone.

She hadn't spent a whole lot of time in the kitchen so it took her several minutes to find a mug then figure out how to use the state-of-the-art microwave. When the milk was warm enough, but not too hot, she took a sip.

Oh, yack!

She screwed up her face. That was awful! She never imagined milk could taste so disgusting. A few heaping spoonfuls of cocoa mix would do the trick, but the last thing she needed was caffeine in her system.

She dumped the milk down the sink, rinsed her cup, then refilled it with apple juice instead.

She considered going back up to her room, but sometimes, when she couldn't sleep, music had a calming effect on her. And she knew for a fact that Ben had a copy of her favorite Van Morrison disk in the stereo cabinet.

She walked to the den, having to almost feel her way through the dark hall, stepped inside and eased the door shut. Rather than switch on the lights, she crossed the dark room and flicked the switch next to the mantle. The gas fireplace sparked to life, bathing the room in warm light.

Next she went to the CD player and, after a bit of fumbling with the millions of little dials and buttons, managed to put Van Morrison in and hit Play. An instant later the bluesy hum of a saxophone filled the room.

Yeah. This would do the trick.

Tess walked over to the fireplace sipping her juice. She wiggled her toes into the soft fur rug, wondering if it was real animal fur. Probably. When it came to decorating the house, Ben's wife hadn't exactly cut corners.

She closed her eyes and let the heat from the fire warm her, the earthy sounds surround her. She swayed to the music, felt her body relaxing, her mind settling. Dancing always did that for her.

She'd once had dreams of being a dancer. It didn't even matter what kind of dancing. She loved it all.

She'd started taking ballet and tap when she was four. She'd been so good that even when her mother couldn't afford to pay, Mrs. Engals, the dance instructor, gave her lessons for free. As she got older she'd worked as Mrs. Engals's assistant, and helped teach the little kids.

She began to view dancing as her ticket out of small town life. She fantasized about getting a full scholarship to Julliard, of performing at Radio City Music Hall in New York. It hadn't even been about the money, although she'd heard the best dancers made tons of it.

She just wanted to get away.

Then, when she was fourteen, she'd been in a car accident with her stepdad. He'd been drunk as usual and hit a tree. She'd been wearing her seatbelt, but as the front end of his crappy little car compressed, her ankle had been crushed by the impact. Three surgeries later she had enough mobility to walk, but her dancing days were over.

It was one more thing her stepdad had stolen from her.

But self-pity was counterproductive, so she swept the negative thoughts away and concentrated on the music, let it carry her away to a place that was peaceful and uncomplicated. Maybe what had attracted her to Ben that night was that he'd asked her to dance.

Well, technically, he hadn't even asked. He'd just locked eyes with her and walked over to where she'd been sitting chatting with the bartender. He'd held out his hand in a silent invitation and without even thinking, she'd taken it, and let him lead her to the dance floor. In her experience most men had two left feet. But Ben pulled her into his arms and they began to move, their bodies in perfect sync. She'd known that instant she would spend the night with him.

It seemed like such a long time ago. So much had changed since then.

Tess closed her eyes and let the music wrap around her. She spun in a circle, letting the thrill of movement wash over her. Her robe swirled around her legs, the orange light from the fire dancing across the silky fabric. She felt dizzy and silly and freer than she had in forever.

God she'd missed this.

The song ended and she heard applause. For a second she thought it was on the CD, then realized it was coming from the other side of the room.

She let out a squeal of surprise and gathered the robe to her chest, squinting into the darkness. "Who's there?"

She saw movement, just an outline at first, then he stepped into the light.

Ben walked slowly toward her wearing a loose pair of flannel pajama bottoms and a hungry smile.

Oh boy.

"You scared me," she said, tucking her robe tighter around her. She suddenly felt so naked, her body too big and ungraceful. "H-how long have you been standing there?"

He didn't answer. His eyes traveled very lazily up her body, from her bare toes all the way to her tousled hair.

Considering the look on his face, *too long*.

As he drew closer and the firelight reached out to grab him, she saw that his pajama bottoms were red. *Red.* He actually owned an article of clothing that wasn't black.

Something about it excited her.

"I'm sorry," she said. "Did I wake you?"

He shook his head, still walking very slowly

toward her. "I couldn't sleep. I was coming down to grab a book and I heard music."

The firelight poured over him, accentuating every inch of his beautifully defined chest, his wide solid shoulders and sinewy arms. Oh my gosh, she'd forgotten how amazing he looked naked.

Not that he was naked, not completely anyway. The rest was best left to her imagination. Although she doubted her memory did him the justice he deserved.

"I didn't know you could dance," he said, still coming closer.

"I don't. I mean, not anymore. I used to, a long time ago." Her back hit the mantle. Only then did she realize, as he was moving toward her, she'd been moving backward.

But her escape route had just disappeared and he was still coming, like an animal on the prowl.

The heat from the fire soaked through the filmy robe, warming her legs, making her feel hot and dizzy. Or maybe it was Ben doing that. She just didn't know anymore.

He closed the space between them, planting his hands against the mantle on either side of her, their bodies not quite touching, but close enough to share heat. And, oh, did he smell delicious. Clean and masculine.

He gazed down at her with penetrating dark eyes. "I promised myself I wouldn't kiss you again. Wouldn't touch you."

What a coincidence. She'd made the same promise to herself. And though a part of her wanted him to touch her and kiss her, another part knew what would happen if he did.

The rational part of her brain recognized what a mistake it would be. Unfortunately she was thinking with the louder, less rational side. The side telling her everything that had happened in the past month had been leading them to this exact moment. That it was fate. Even though she didn't believe in it. A person made their own destiny, determined their own future.

Of course that didn't mean a person wouldn't make a few careless mistakes in the process.

"Do you ever think about that night?" he asked, his eyes searching her face.

Only constantly. Like, what would have happened if she'd stayed? What if the condom hadn't failed?

What did it matter now?

Ben's eyes locked on hers, so full of desire and affection. She shivered with excitement and anticipation. She hadn't even realized until now just how badly she wanted him to kiss her.

"We shouldn't," he said, but he was already dipping his head, and she was rising up on her toes to meet him halfway.

"No, we shouldn't," she agreed. "But let's do it anyway."

Eight

It never ceased to amaze Tess how thrilling it could be kissing this man. When their lips met, she went weak all over.

It was hot and deep and passionate, as if they were making up for lost time. His hands cupped her face, guiding her head to the perfect angle, and she tangled hers in his hair. His bare chest felt hot and powerful through the thin cotton nightgown. His arms caging her, the way he assumed control, was as exciting as it was scary.

This wasn't just a kiss, this was a possession, and she could do little more than cling for dear life and enjoy the ride. At that moment he owned her, body, mind and soul, and like a fool she gave herself willingly.

When he finally broke the kiss, they were both flushed and breathing hard.

"We shouldn't be doing this," he said in a husky whisper, just before he captured her mouth and started all over again.

She felt reckless and irresponsible, and the worst part was, she liked it.

Then Ben was undressing her. Her robe went first, and as it fell to the floor he began kissing all the skin he'd exposed. Her shoulders and throat. The ridge of her collarbone.

He nibbled and licked his way back to her mouth while his hands continued their quest for bare flesh, tugging the straps of her gown down over her arms. In a few short seconds she was going to be naked.

"Mrs. Smith," she mumbled. "What if she—"

"The door is locked."

His housekeeper may have been as frigid as an iceberg, but she wasn't stupid. "If she wakes up, she's going to know exactly what we're doing."

He looked down at her, his eyes black with lust. "Do I look like I care?"

For reasons she didn't understand, the fact that he wasn't interested in hiding this, made her want him that much more. Besides, her brain was so fuzzy at this point it wasn't as if she could tell him to stop.

Ben tugged the gown down, somehow managing to be tender and commanding at the same time. He eased her against him and she shuddered when the sensitive tips of her breasts brushed his bare chest. Heat from the fire made her skin feel warm and tingly.

She didn't know if it was hormones or the fact that it had been so long, but she felt as if she were drowning, being sucked under by waves of arousal. And she let it happen.

"You taste like apples," he rasped against her lips, and kissed her deeper, as if he were trying to steal the flavor from her mouth.

Her panties were the next thing to go, then he just looked at her, his eyes roaming slowly and deliberately over her body. She wondered if her over-accentuated shape would turn him off, if seeing her bare belly would bother him.

If it had, he didn't let it show. And since she didn't want to be the only one naked, she took a great deal of satisfaction in liberating him from the pajama bottoms.

Ben eased her to the floor and they stretched out beside one another on the rug. There was more kissing and touching, slower this time. Sort of lazy and sweet, as if the urgency was gone. This was going to happen so there was no need to rush, no reason not to take their time relearning all the wonderful, sinfully erotic places they had discovered that first night. Her body had never responded so effortlessly, so fiercely to a man's touch. Something about this, about being with him, was so right.

And so very wrong—which made it that much more exciting.

"Talk to me," he said. "Tell me what you want."

"Anything," she said breathlessly. "Everything."

Eyes on her face, he slipped a hand between her thighs, teasing her with featherlight caresses. "Like this?"

"Yes." Exactly like that. But when she reached down to touch him, to stroke him just like he was stroking her, he brushed her hand aside.

"You'll get your turn later," he said. "Right now, I want to make you feel good."

"I want to make you feel good, too." She tried again but this time he caught her wrist in his hand and pinned her arm to the rug over her head.

"This does make me feel good." He lowered his head and sucked a nipple into his mouth. She felt the warm, wet pull of arousal, the zing of sensation travel all the way down between her thighs, to the place where his fingers explored and played, sinking deeper into the slippery folds of skin. She moaned and closed her eyes. "I wonder if you taste as good as you feel."

He began licking and nibbling his way down her body, pressing her thighs apart, and she knew he intended to find out. It seemed to take him *forever* to reach his destination, like he had all the time in the world. And by the time he took that first taste, when she felt the sweep of his tongue, she was wound so tightly her body arched up against his mouth. She didn't think it got any better than this...until he zeroed in on the little tangle of nerves. She cried out at the intense jolt of pleasure. Everything began to clench and almost instantly she was coming.

And coming…and coming.

"Wow," she breathed when it was over, her body as limp as a wet noodle. *"Wow."*

"As much as I'd love to take credit for that, I think it had more to do with hormones than skill." He kissed his way back up her body until they were lying side by side again.

"I've been wondering something, too," she said.

"What's that?"

"What *you* taste like."

He flashed her that sexy simmering grin as she pushed him onto his back, and tortured him in the same slow, lazy way he had her. Until the urge to make love to him, the need for him to be inside her was too great to resist.

As she straddled his hips and eased herself down, taking him deep inside of her, never had anything felt so right. So perfect. She lost all sense of time, all sense of herself. All that mattered was this moment. Making love to Ben was as simple as it was complex, as sweet as it was erotic.

She linked her hands through Ben's and pinned them on either side of his head, driving herself hard against him, over and over until he gasped and arched.

He looked up at her, his eyes glassy and unfocused and whispered her name, *"Tess,"* then the grip on her hands tightened and every part of him began to tense.

The sensation brought her to an entirely new level of ecstasy. She threw her head back and cried out as her body clenched tight around him, and for that brief moment everything in her world was painfully perfect. This was the way it should always be, this feeling of connection.

Ben pulled her into his arms and just held her. For several minutes they didn't speak. They just lay there quietly, arms and legs entwined, touching and stroking.

She snuggled against him, her head resting on his arm. "Say something to me in Spanish."

"Like what?"

"I don't know, anything."

"Su belleza elimina mi respiración," he said with perfect inflection.

She sighed contentedly. She didn't know what it was she found so sexy about him speaking a foreign language. "What does that mean?"

"My arm is falling asleep."

She laughed and poked him in the side. "No, it doesn't. I think *respiración* is respiration, and I'm pretty sure *belleza* is beauty. So what, I have beautiful lungs?"

"I said, your beauty takes my breath away." He rolled her onto her back and gazed down at her, searching her face. He kissed her forehead, the tip of her nose. "What are we doing, Tess?"

"I don't know, but we do it really well."

"We didn't use protection."

"It's not like I can get any more pregnant than I already am."

"Good point."

She looped her arms around his neck. God, she loved touching him. Being close to him. "Maybe this is just something we needed to do, you know, to get it out of our systems."

"Yeah, maybe."

"And if we do it a lot, by the time I have to leave, I'm sure we'll be completely sick of each other."

The corner of his mouth crept up. "How much is a lot?"

"As much as it takes, I guess." Although, she couldn't imagine herself getting tired of this. Getting tired of him. Ever. "What about Mrs. Smith?"

"She's really not my type."

Tess laughed. "What I mean is, unless we're extremely discreet, she's going to notice sooner or later."

"I told you earlier, I don't care if she notices. We're consenting adults. What we do is our business."

This had disaster written all over it. A pinkie bandage on a wound that required stitches—or amputation. But right now she was happy, and that was so rare these days that she was willing to hang on to the feeling, whatever the cost.

He was giving her that drowsy-eyed, hungry look again that made her feel warm and tingly all over. Looks like they were going to work on getting sick of each other right now.

She pulled him down for a kiss and their bodies settled together. Even with her tummy in the way, they were a perfect fit. Though she knew that soon enough she would be so big, lying this close in this position would be impossible. They would just have to find more imaginative ways to get close.

It was at that exact second that it happened. She felt a very distinct jolt dead center in her stomach. The baby's first kick.

She gasped with surprise and looked up at Ben. "Did you feel that?"

He'd felt it. She knew the instant she saw his face.

She wasn't sure what she'd been expecting. She knew excitement at feeling his baby move was a lot to ask for given the circumstances. Instead he looked like he might be sick.

And suddenly, she felt exactly the same way.

Until that moment it hadn't been truly clear to her, she hadn't been able to wrap her mind around the concept of just how much he didn't want this baby. And realizing that, seeing it for herself, sucked every bit of joy out of what should have been the happiest moment of her life.

Her arms dropped from around his neck and he rolled away, sitting up on the rug, his back to her. All she could do was curl into a ball and close her eyes against the bitter and acute pain in her heart.

His baby kicked, and rather than feeling happy, he was devastated.

"I'm sorry," he said.

She shivered. She suddenly felt so cold, all the way through her skin and deep down to the bone. Cold and vulnerable and rubbed raw.

She grabbed her robe from where it had dropped

on the floor and covered herself with it. It was hot from the fire, but even that didn't chase away the chill. She felt as if she might never be warm again.

"I should go," Ben said.

She couldn't answer, not without him hearing how completely torn up she felt inside.

He sat there for several seconds, then he got up, pulled on his pajamas and left.

She waited for the tears to come, for the grief to swallow her up, but she just felt numb. Cold and hollow and alone.

She would just have to get used to this, learn to live with it. At least as long as she was living in Ben's house, carrying his child.

Or maybe it would be this way for the rest of her life.

Ben stared out his office window, into the cold, rainy gloom, thinking that it was a perfect complement to his lousy mood.

He felt like such a jerk.

He shouldn't have left Tess alone, but there was no way he could sit there and pretend everything was okay, pretend that feeling his baby kick hadn't made him sick inside. It hadn't really hit him until then, hadn't truly been real until he'd felt it move, that it was his baby growing inside her. His flesh and blood.

It was so damned unfair. Why did this baby deserve to live when his son hadn't been given a chance? And why did his heart ache to love it when he knew that was impossible?

He didn't even have the guts to go talk to her. He had no idea what to say—how to explain. That feeble I'm sorry he'd left her with last night just wasn't going to cut it.

His office door opened and he turned to find Mrs. Smith standing there. When Tess hadn't eaten breakfast and didn't show up for lunch or dinner, he'd finally sent his housekeeper up to check on her.

"Is she awake?"

"She's still in bed. She said she's not feeling well, but that you shouldn't worry."

Like him, she probably hadn't slept last night. He'd tossed and turned, finally giving up and rolling out of bed with the sun. He turned back to the window. "Thank you."

"She looked as if she'd been crying," Mrs. Smith said, and Ben winced. He'd assumed she would be, but to know for sure, and to know it was his fault, was a million times more horrible.

"Would you like to talk about it?"

"Talk about what?"

"Whatever it is that's wrong."

What could he possibly say that Mrs. Smith would understand?

"Your mother called again this morning. She knows something is up. I'm running out of excuses. At some point you'll have to tell her what's going on."

"I will." When he was ready. When he was sure what was going on.

"You know," she said softly, "I lost a son, too."

He spun around to face her. "What? When?"

"He was a soldier in Vietnam. He was killed two days before his nineteenth birthday."

"I'm sorry," he said, not because he thought it would make her feel better. He just didn't know what else to say.

"Five years later my husband passed from cancer. That was the year I came to work for your family."

She looked so sad, and Ben could only stare at her, unable to comprehend what she was telling him. He hadn't even known she was married. Why hadn't he heard about this before?

She had a life, a history that he knew nothing about. It also explained why, as good as she was to him, he'd always felt as though she kept him at arm's length. He used to think it just her personality. Now he wasn't so sure. "Why didn't you ever tell me this?"

"To talk about it, would be acknowledging that it happened. That wouldn't bring them back. Would it?"

"So what, you just pretend they didn't exist?"

"The way Jeanette and your son no longer exist?"

She had no right to judge him. She had no clue what went on in his head. "Not a day goes by—not an hour—that I don't think about them. And miss them."

"Maybe that's your problem."

She wasn't making any sense. He was supposed to acknowledge them, but not think about them? Not miss them?

"You should go talk to Tess," Mrs. Smith said.

"I can't."

"You mean you won't." She shook her head sadly. "I hate to see you making the same mistakes I did."

He wasn't making a mistake. He was avoiding one.

He turned back to the window. He didn't think it was possible, but he felt even worse than he had before.

Nine

Tess gave herself a full day to wallow in self-pity. All Saturday she stayed in bed. And she must have looked pretty terrible, because even Mrs. Smith had been less snippy than usual. She'd come up to check on Tess and offered to bring her tea and toast to settle her stomach, when what Tess really needed was a gigantic bandage to slap over her chest. To seal the wound where Ben had reached in and ripped out her heart.

But by Sunday afternoon the self-indulgence was getting old and most likely induced by hormones more than anything else. The only thing she could do was get over it. She couldn't hide away any longer, and she had to stop feeling sorry for herself.

If she'd shut down every time something bad had happened to her, she would have stopped living a long time ago.

Maybe the real problem here was that she'd finally let herself admit something she'd been denying for months.

She loved Ben.

She'd fallen in love with him that night in the resort. Maybe not in the soul deep way that developed over time. But they had scratched the surface of something bigger. Something profound.

The question was, how could she love a man who would deny his own child? The baby they had created together. Maybe because in her heart and soul she knew he was a good person who had just been deeply hurt and hadn't yet bounced back.

At least, that was what she was trying to convince herself.

When she told him she considered him a friend, that had been a lie. Or at the very least a major understatement. What she felt for him went far beyond friendship. Far beyond anything she had ever experienced in a relationship. And in four months it would end.

Unless she could do something to change his mind.

It wasn't the first time her mind had entertained the thought. She'd been tiptoeing around the idea for days, not willing to let it take root. Because she knew that there was a very real possibility she would end up hurting and alone if it backfired.

She was just getting ready to venture downstairs

to find Ben when there was a knock at her door. It was probably Mrs. Smith, coming to get her lunch tray.

She swung the door open, but it was Ben standing in the hallway.

She could play this two ways. She could act indignant and try to make him feel badly for the way he had treated her, which would probably only make things more uncomfortable between them, or she could accept things for what they were, and make the best of the time they had together.

She smiled. "Hi."

"Hi." For a minute he just looked at her, probably trying to decide if she was mad at him. Then he asked, "Are you feeling better?"

She turned up the wattage on her smile. Even if she wanted to, she couldn't stay mad at him. He didn't mean to hurt her. He cared about her. She knew he did. She couldn't ask for more than he was able to give. More than he was capable of. "Much better, thanks."

He just stood there, hands in his pants pockets, and she realized, he was waiting to be invited in. She hoped this wasn't like the vampire books she used to read when she was a kid. Once you invited a vampire in, you were toast.

He was so dark and handsome, if she hadn't already seen him in the sun, she might have been worried. But Ben was as mortal as they came.

"Would you like to come in?" She opened the door wider and he stepped past her into the sitting room. The second she shut the door his arms were around her. He pulled her to him and just held her.

"I'm sorry," he said.

She sighed and pressed her cheek against his chest, breathed in the spicy scent of his cologne. He smelled warm and familiar. "Me, too."

He held her tighter. "I missed you."

She felt like laughing and crying all at once. "I missed you, too."

"Should we talk about it?"

That was the one thing that she *didn't* want to talk about, or even worse analyze to death. She just wanted to forget it had ever happened. "I understand the way things are. I just…it caught me by surprise, I guess."

He nodded. "Me, too."

"So if it happens again we'll be prepared."

"Exactly," he agreed. Then he smiled down at her and she could tell everything was going to be okay. They were past the awkwardness.

Then the baby kicked. Just like the other night. Plenty hard for Ben to feel it, too. She held her breath, waiting for him to back away.

He didn't.

"Does that happen a lot now?" he asked instead.

"Just since the other night."

"That night was the first time?"

"Yep."

He swore under his breath. "And I ruined it, didn't I?"

"It's not your fault."

He cupped her chin with his palm and lifted her face so he could meet her eyes. "Why do you put up with me?"

Because I love you, she was tempted to say. Instead she shrugged. "Beats me."

"Me, too." He studied her face, as if the answer was there somewhere. Then his eyes wandered down to her mouth and she knew exactly what he was thinking. He wanted to kiss her. And she wanted him to.

"You look tired," he said.

"I do?" She didn't *feel* tired. She'd practically slept all day yesterday. "I'm fine, really."

"No, really, you look exhausted." He flashed her that sizzling, seductive grin then leaned back and locked the door to her suite. "I think you need to take a nap."

Oh—a *nap*.

She could tell by his smile, this *nap* wouldn't involve sleep. "Come to think of it, I am a little drowsy. Maybe a quick nap wouldn't be a bad idea."

"I think a long nap would be better." He started walking backward toward the bedroom, pulling her along with him. "I'll tuck you in."

He led them into the bedroom, already working the buttons on her blouse. The drapes were drawn and the room had a hazy, dim look, like stepping into the middle of a dream.

He eased her shirt down her arms and let it drop to the floor then unhooked her bra. She'd never been terribly aggressive or confident when it came to sex, but Ben seemed to draw out the vixen in her. She tugged his shirt up over his head and flung it behind her, then went to work on his belt.

She didn't think anything could top making love on a rug in front of the fire, but just being with Ben, no matter where they were, felt special. It wasn't easy to forget all that they couldn't be together. Instead, as they caressed and kissed, loved each other in that sweet, effortless way, she felt as if she were exactly where she belonged. Even if that was only for five minutes, or an hour. Maybe, in the long run, all these little pieces of perfection would add up to something bigger. Something neither of them expected.

And if it didn't, the time that they did have together would just have to be enough.

They tumbled into bed together and snuggled up under the comforter. Ben stroked her skin, exploring every hill and crevice, his touch leisurely and sweet one minute, shockingly intimate the next. She loved the feeling of his hands exploring her, but she loved it even more when he used his mouth. He licked and nipped, here and there, as if she were his favorite snack and he didn't want to devour her too quickly. Somehow he managed to make every stroke, every touch feel as thrilling and new as the first time.

"I love the way you taste," he said, nibbling her throat, running his tongue lightly along the cleft between her breasts, making her whole body sizzle with desire. "What do you want Tess? Just tell me and I'll do it."

She didn't have to tell him. He was always able

to anticipate exactly what she craved, what she needed, but there was something erotic and forbidden about saying the words out loud. And she wouldn't dare deny him the pleasure of hearing them, not when he went far and above the call of duty to make her feel good. Gave her at least two orgasms to his one. Sometimes more.

So she told him, in very blatant, explicit language, exactly what she wanted, and how she wanted it.

"Damn," he said, shaking his head, but she could tell he loved it. "I'd love to, but are you sure I won't hurt you?"

"I'm sure," she said, and the next thing she knew, she was flat on her back, thighs pressed wide and Ben was burying himself deep inside her, just as hard and fast as she asked him to. She went from being aroused to…well, something she'd never felt before. Something bigger than herself, bigger than both of them together. It overwhelmed her body and when her skin could no longer contain all that sensation it radiated out, expanding and flexing and growing. She knew she was making noise, moaning and thrashing and digging her fingernails into his backside, raking them down his arms. Someone could have heard, but she was too far gone to care.

Ben hooked both of his arms behind her knees, easing them as far back as they would go and, eyes locked on her face, sank deep inside her. Deeper than any man had ever been. And with no warning at all, everything peaked and something inside her exploded. It filled her with a feeling, a sensation she couldn't even describe, something along the lines of ecstasy. Or nirvana.

As she slowly came back to herself, she looked up to find Ben gazing down at her, a perplexed look on his face.

"What was that?"

"I'm not sure," she said with a lazy smile, tangling her fingers in his hair and pulling him down for a kiss. "But give me a minute to catch my breath and we can do it again."

They *napped* for several hours on and off until dinner, which they ate naked in bed. In lieu of dessert they took another long nap, shared a shower, then lay in bed, their bodies tangled together, and just talked.

"Tell me about Jeanette," Tess said, rising up on one elbow to look at him, her belly pressed into the dip of his hip. "What was she like?"

"Colorful," Ben said, idly toying with a lock of her hair. "And spoiled, and complicated. But fun. And she was probably the most driven woman I've ever met. Her career meant everything to her. Come to think of it, she was a lot like my mother in that respect." He shifted on his side to face her. "What about you? Any significant romances? Besides the pool table kiss?"

"Not really. I have a gift for finding men who are bad for me. I think I inherited that from my mom."

"There must have been someone special."

"There was this boy in high school. David Fischer. He was a real sweetheart. But then I had to drop out of school and get a full time job, so that pretty much killed that."

"Why did you need a full-time job?"

"To pay rent. I couldn't stay in my stepdad's house any longer."

Ben frowned. "There was abuse?"

She shrugged. "The physical and emotional stuff. It was just a regular part of life. I was used to it. But then he started...*looking* at me."

His frown deepened. "Looking at you how?"

"With that look men get when they want something from you. I told my mom and she accused me of being selfish. I knew it was only a matter of time before he tried something, and I obviously wasn't going to get any help from her, so I packed up my stuff and left. She didn't even try to stop me. I've been on my own ever since."

That she'd been through something so horrible made Ben sick to his stomach. Her mother, the one person she should have been able to depend on, had let her down. It's a wonder she could trust at all.

"My parents might not have been around much, but they made sure I was well taken care of." He reached up and brushed the hair back from Tess's face, tucking it behind her ear. She was so pretty. So soft and gentle. But strong. Stronger than even he had realized. "Did your real dad know anything about this? Didn't he do anything?"

"This is a man who signed away all his parental rights so he could get out of paying child support. And it's not like he couldn't afford it. He didn't want anything to do with me."

Ben hated that she'd been through such hell, only to be rejected all over again by him. He hated that she accepted this kind of treatment as normal. Didn't she know that she deserved so much more?

She should be with someone who accepted her child. And maybe someday she would be. She was only twenty-five. She could meet a decent guy who would raise Ben's baby and be a good husband to Tess. He wanted that for her.

So why did the idea make his chest hurt? He couldn't be a father to this child. Not even if he wanted to. But he didn't want anyone else to be, either. He couldn't have it both ways.

It was as if there was some sort of barrier blocking the part of his heart that used to long for a family. Either that, or maybe it had just shriveled up and died.

And he knew the whole concept of sleeping together until they got sick of each other was just his way of justifying what they were doing. He wasn't going to get sick of her. If it weren't for the baby, he didn't doubt that he would eventually be down on one knee asking her to marry him.

He'd loved Jeanette. Their marriage had been good in a hectic, complicated way. But he and Tess had something different. Something easy and satisfying, and so deep they'd barely scratched the surface. Being with Tess had been like coming home. A safe, warm, comfortable place. A place where he could see himself putting down roots.

And because of him, they would never get the chance. He'd thought maybe, just maybe, he could make it work. Maybe he could get used to being around the baby. He'd been pretty much ignored by his parents as a child and he'd turned out okay.

The weird thing was, he couldn't do that. He wanted the baby to have everything he didn't. He wanted better for it. Two parents who loved and adored it, not one who merely tolerated its presence.

Besides, he knew Tess would never allow it. When it came to the baby, she didn't compromise. She expected better.

And she *deserved* it.

When Ben woke the following morning, he was still sprawled on Tess's bed. He reached over to find her, but the spot beside him was empty, the sheets cool. He hadn't meant to spend the night. They'd sat up late talking, and when Tess had drifted off to sleep, Ben just lay there watching her. Five more minutes, he kept telling himself. Five more minutes and he would go to his own room. He must have drifted off.

He couldn't help thinking that staying here had been a mistake. That Tess might get the wrong idea. He didn't want to mislead her into thinking anything had changed. Sleeping together was intimate enough, but to spend the night together?

He sat up in bed, stretching and rubbing the sleep from his eyes. He looked over at the digital clock and saw that it was eight-thirty. Much later than he usually slept in. From the vicinity of the bathroom he heard off-key humming. A second later Tess appeared, looking far too chipper and awake for someone who couldn't have gotten more than four or five hours of sleep.

When she saw him sitting there, she gave him one of those bright smiles. She looked so…*happy.* "Good morning."

"'Morning. You're up early."

"I would have slept in, but I have to go to the doctor."

"What's wrong?" he snapped, cringing when he realized how harshly the words had come out.

Tess was incredibly patient with him. "Nothing. It's just time for my monthly checkup. Six months already."

He shoved his hair back from his face. What was wrong with him that he automatically assumed the worst? He knew monthly visits were part of the routine. It's not as if he hadn't been through this before. And though he'd never written down her due date or kept track of her pregnancy, his internal calendar wouldn't let him forget.

"I'm sorry. I didn't mean to snap."

She just gave him that sweet, understanding smile. "It's okay. It'll just take time."

No, it wasn't okay. He had to stop overreacting, stop worrying so much.

She sat on the edge of the bed beside him. "I was kinda surprised that you were still here this morning."

"Yeah, me, too."

"In case you're wondering, I realize nothing has changed."

Leave it to Tess to come right out and say exactly what she was feeling. "That doesn't bother you?"

"If I had any expectation that this relationship had even a slim chance of surviving it might have, but I prefer to live in the real world."

If he really cared about her, he would end this right here, right now. He was only going to end up hurting her. And the longer they kept this up, the worse it would be for both of them. But he was selfish. He wanted her for as long as he could have her.

He wasn't ready to let go.

"I'm going to do some shopping after my appointment, so I probably won't be back for a while." She leaned over and kissed his cheek, as naturally as if they had been doing this for years. "See you later."

"Drive safe." He waited until she'd left, then fell back onto the bed.

How did people do it? How did couples who had lost a baby make it through subsequent pregnancies without going insane with worry?

Tess wasn't out of the woods yet. If something were to happen and she had the baby now, odds were likely it wouldn't survive, or if it did, it could be severely handicapped. Blind or mentally disabled.

Tess was wrong. Time wasn't going to fix this.

If nothing else, it would only get worse.

Ten

Tess sat in the waiting room of the doctor's office, feeling confused and more than a little frustrated. Last night had been…incredible. She'd never felt so close to a man—to *anyone*. She'd never shared so many intimate secrets. She'd told him things about herself that she'd never told another living soul. She'd thought for sure that he would be gone in the morning. Then she'd opened her eyes and there he lay, sleeping soundly. Looking gorgeous of course.

And like an idiot, she'd almost let herself believe that it meant something. That something had changed.

Then he'd flipped out when she said she was going to the doctor and they were back to square one.

Back to the realization that this relationship was not long-term.

She should have ended it right there. She should have told him it would be best if they stopped while they were ahead and parted as friends. But she was selfish. She wanted as much time with him as she could get. Besides, there was always the chance that the longer she knew him, she would discover he had some annoying habit she couldn't stand to live with. Like, maybe he bit his nails—or even worse, his toenails. Or picked his teeth at the dinner table—or his nose.

It was a long shot.

Tess was called into the examining room, and the doctor sufficiently poked and prodded her belly, taking measurements and listening to the baby's heartbeat. Which was fast, meaning it may or may not be a girl…or a squid for all she knew. After receiving a clean bill of health, she dressed, then made her next month's appointment. But as she headed out to the car, she had the eerie sensation that someone was watching her. She stopped and scanned either side of the street, watching the people—mostly tourists—moving around her.

No one seemed to be paying attention to her, or even looked the least bit suspicious. She figured Ben's paranoia must have been rubbing off on her, and determined not to worry about it. But as she walked to her car later that afternoon, her arms filled with bags, she had that same sensation of being watched.

She dropped the bags in the trunk and climbed in the driver's seat, keeping an eye on the rearview mirror as she drove home, but if someone had followed her, they kept themselves well hidden.

When she got back she pulled into the garage and headed inside with her purchases, running into Mrs. Smith on her way through the kitchen. She sat in the breakfast nook, making a list on a yellow pad of paper. Her writing was small and neat, just what Tess would have expected from a woman like her.

"I'm going grocery shopping tomorrow," Mrs. Smith informed her. "Do you need anything while I'm out?"

Tess was so stunned by the offer she nearly swallowed her own tongue. Mrs. Smith had to have known Tess and Ben spent the night together. Tess had been anticipating hostility, not an offer to run errands.

For the life of her, she would never understand Mrs. Smith.

"I don't think so, but thanks for offering."

She gestured to the bags Tess was carrying. "Do you need help with those?"

Wow, now an offer to help? She gave the woman a scrutinizing look. "Who are you and what have you done with Mrs. Smith?"

She got a look of exasperation in return.

"I've got them, thanks. Do you know if Ben is in his office?"

"I believe he's upstairs in his suite."

Tess waited for a warning that he didn't want to

be bothered, or that Tess was forbidden to enter his private domain, but she just went back to her list.

Okay. She was really creeping Tess out.

As she walked to the stairs something else struck her as odd. Light. There was light and color everywhere. Someone had opened the curtains in the front room. She circled through the entire lower floor, going from room to room, finding each one flooded with sunshine, until she ended up back in the kitchen, still clutching all the bags.

Mrs. Smith gave her an odd look. "Are you lost?"

"No, I just…the curtains are all open."

She looked at Tess questioningly. "Yes?"

Like an explanation was too much to ask for? "Oh, never mind."

She headed up the stairs instead, to Ben's suite, bags in tow, and knocked on the door. When she didn't get an answer, she considered going back to her own room to wait for him, but she was too excited.

She knocked louder, and when he still didn't answer, she opened the door and peeked her head inside. Would he mind if she entered unannounced?

The sitting room was set up much like her own, only flopped the opposite way and decorated in darker, richer hues. Definitely more masculine, but without being too overpowering. It even smelled masculine. Ben's own unique scent. And surprisingly enough, the drapes were wide open, displaying the same breathtaking view of the garden as her room.

What was going on?

She hesitated on the threshold, still unsure of how he would feel about her being in his suite. Maybe that was a line in their relationship he wasn't willing to cross.

"Yoo-hoo!" she called. "Anybody here?"

"Come on in," she heard him answer. "I'm in the bedroom."

Or he wouldn't mind at all.

She pushed her way inside and shut the door behind her. She stepped into the bedroom just as Ben appeared from the closet, his hair wet and dripping, a dark blue towel riding low on his slim hips, his chest glistening with moisture.

"Hi," he said, shooting her a grin, not at all bothered by the fact that she had infiltrated his private space. He was also completely at ease being mostly naked in front of her. Not that he shouldn't be, especially after last night. She'd been up close and personal with just about every part of his body. And as many times as she'd seen it lately, it still took her breath away and made her knees feel gooey.

He gestured to her bags. "It looks as if someone had a successful shopping trip."

"It was. I got you a present. Actually, quite a few presents."

"You didn't have to buy me anything," he said, but the look on his face suggested it had been a long time since anyone had bought him a present and he was the teensiest bit curious as to what it could be.

"Now, I want you to keep an open mind," she said.

"Uh-oh. That's usually not a good sign."

"It's nothing bad, I promise." She walked over to the bed and dumped the contents of the bags out onto the comforter. "I was going to start you out slowly with a shirt or two, but there were some awesome clearance sales. I got a bit carried away."

"I guess," Ben said, staring at the clothes piled there. Colorful clothes.

Shirts and pants and even boxers. And not a single black item.

Ben picked up a polo shirt the same creamy beige as the carpet and looked at the tag on the collar. "Out of curiosity, how did you know what size to buy?"

"I peeked at the tags on your clothes yesterday."

He laid the shirt across the bed with the others. "So, you've been planning this, have you?"

"Just for a day or two." She'd worried he might be angry with her, that maybe this was crossing some invisible line in the sand that he'd drawn. Instead he looked almost…amused. "I know you like to wear black—"

"The truth is, I don't. It doesn't matter to me one way or the other. That just happens to be all I own."

She shot him a disbelieving look.

"See for yourself," he said and she followed him into his closet. And damned if he wasn't telling the truth. Row upon row of black.

"I have the fashion sense of a brick. I just wear

whatever is there. Jeanette pretty much did all my shopping, and she liked me in black. Then she didn't have to worry about me wearing clothes she considered mismatched or out of fashion. She was very much into appearances."

"Well, now you have colorful clothes," she said feeling relief and a tiny bit of pride. "Anything you don't like I can return."

"I'm sure I'll like it all," he said.

A corner of fabric peeking out from a partially open drawer caught her eye. Fabric that was not only not black, but also incredibly familiar.

She walked over to the drawer and yanked it open, then looked up at Ben who was grinning from ear to ear, and didn't seem to care that she was going through his things. Or more to the point, *her* things. "My clothes!"

They were all folded and tucked neatly away. She sorted through them and as far as she could tell everything was there. "You said you burned them."

Ben leaned in the doorway and folded his thick arms across that beautifully defined chest. He looked like a *Playgirl* centerfold. "No, *you* said I burned them. I just didn't tell you that you were wrong. I knew if you believed they were still recoverable, you never would have agreed to buy new clothes."

"Oh," she said, shaking her head. "You're evil."

He grinned. "Yeah, I am," he agreed, looking awfully proud of himself. "But it worked, didn't it?"

Yeah, it worked. "Just like you let me believe you were an alcoholic. Which I know now that you aren't."

"If I had told you I wasn't, would you have believed me?"

He was right. She probably wouldn't have.

"You were going to believe what you wanted to believe," he said. "And that's okay. I knew I would have to earn your trust. It wasn't a lot to ask."

"Just so we're clear, if you don't like the clothes I bought you, don't be afraid to say so. It won't hurt my feelings." At least, not too much.

"I love it all," he said.

"But you haven't even looked at most of it."

"Doesn't matter. It's from you."

That was one of the sweetest things anyone had ever said to her. Especially since technically, they were really from himself. He'd be paying the bill. She'd only picked them out.

"How did your appointment go?" he asked.

"I'm right on schedule." She could see that talking about it made him uncomfortable, so she left it at that. She gave him credit for even asking. No need to torture him with details he didn't want. "Do you have to work?"

"Not necessarily." Pushing off from the door frame he walked slowly toward her. "That shopping probably took a lot out of you, huh?"

"No, not really."

"I think it did. You look awfully tired."

Oh boy, he had that look. That sizzling predatory grin. They were going to play the nap game again.

A grin curled her mouth. "Yeah, you're right, I'm *completely* exhausted."

"I thought you were."

He dropped his towel and had her out of her clothes and under the covers in a minute flat. They made love most of the afternoon, had dinner, watched a movie, then had another *nap* in Ben's room before bed. She'd had more sex in the past couple of days than she had had in the last five years. They just couldn't seem to get enough of each other.

"Maybe I should go," she told Ben around midnight, when she was getting too sleepy to keep her eyes open. She didn't want him to be uncomfortable, or feel as if he had to let her stay because he had last night.

Instead of letting go, his arm closed tightly around her. "No. I want you to stay."

That was all she needed to hear. She burrowed under the covers, cuddling against him. If it ended tomorrow, at least they would have had this final night together. That was all they could do, live as if each day together might be their last.

Ben had a serious problem.

He'd realized it this morning when, like every morning for the past two weeks, he woke with Tess naked, soft and warm in his arms. It became clear the instant she looked up at him with a sleepy smile.

When he couldn't stop himself from touching her. When he didn't feel complete until he'd buried himself deep inside her.

He was falling in love with her.

A lazy, wistful, effortless kind of love that felt as natural to him as breathing. He wanted to marry her, and wake up with her every morning for the rest of his life. He knew it would be everything his first marriage hadn't been.

He'd loved Jeanette, but Tess was his soul mate.

But what he didn't want was her baby.

It didn't escape him what a complete bastard he was, what a horrible person he'd become for not wanting his own child. It wasn't even so much that he didn't *want* the baby or that he didn't *care*. He did care—too much—which is why he knew it would never work. His heart wouldn't let it happen.

"Have you got a minute?"

Ben turned to find Mrs. Smith standing in his office doorway. He'd grown accustomed to keeping it open. When he did shut it now, he felt closed off and isolated. Same with the windows. Where he used to prefer the darkness—the peace it brought him—now he craved the light. He'd even begun taking walks with Tess in the mornings and sometimes again in the evening. The days were longer now, the weather pleasantly warm.

"Sure, come on in."

Mrs. Smith walked into his office, a magazine clutched in her hand, looking very unsettled about something. "You have a problem."

Ben couldn't help laughing. He had more than one problem. He had a list as long as his arm. "Tell me something I didn't already know."

"I was in line at the grocery store when I saw this." She handed him the magazine. A gossip rag.

He read the cover and cursed under his breath—a harsh four letter word that would have earned him a mouth full of soap when he was a kid. "I guess I should have expected this."

"There's more inside."

He opened it, cringed and said, "Aw, hell."

"I take it you haven't looked out front."

"Not yet. Don't tell me…"

"There are at least twenty. Mostly local. A few cable. Word is going to spread fast."

Damn.

This was not something he had wanted to deal with. Not something he wanted Tess to have to deal with. "I should warn Tess."

He grabbed the magazine and pushed himself up from his chair. He left his office, stopping to peer out the front window—*damn*—then went off to look for Tess. He found her in the library curled up in the chaise by the window reading a book.

When she saw him, she gave him a bright smile. "Hi."

"Hey. We need to talk."

Worry crinkled her forehead. "Okay."

"We have a problem," he said.

No kidding, Tess thought. In fact, they had more than one.

Ben handed her a magazine.

"What's this?" Her heart sank as the headline screamed at her in bold letters, Millionaire Widower's Pregnant Mistress!

Underneath it was a photo of her coming out of the doctor's office, looking very pregnant and glancing around guiltily, as if she had something to hide.

So she'd been right. Someone had been following her.

"There's more inside," he said.

She opened the paper and there were more pictures. A few of her in town shopping and another of her driving up to Ben's house, the address clearly visible by the gate. Beside a column of type she was sure she would be better off not reading, there was a photo of Ben and his wife, a gorgeous Hollywood couple, and a shot of Ben in a dark suit getting out of a limo at what Tess could only assume was the funeral.

She shut the magazine. "Wonderful."

"There's more," Ben said.

"More?" How could this possibly get any worse?

"The press is camped out in front of the house."

Oh, yeah, that *was* worse. She muttered a curse under her breath.

"My sentiments exactly," Ben said. "By law they can't enter the property. Although that doesn't always stop them. And it doesn't stop them from using a telephoto lens."

"What should we do?"

He shrugged. "Not much we can do. Just wait it out. If you don't want to have to talk to them, or see your picture in the paper, I wouldn't plan on going anywhere for a while. That includes the garden. And don't get too close to any open windows at night."

"How long?"

"No way to tell. Probably until the next big scandal hits."

Swell. "I'm really sorry."

"How is this your fault? I'm the one who's sorry. I'm used to this kind of thing. You're not."

She sat on the love seat. Morbid curiosity got the best of her and she skimmed the article. Ben sat on the arm and read over her shoulder.

"The worst part is that nothing they printed is untrue. Not totally at least. I'm your mistress and I'm definitely pregnant."

"Tess, you and I both know that you are a hell of a lot more to me than a mistress."

She handed the magazine back to him. "I can't look at this anymore."

"What you need to understand," Ben said, "is that this will probably get a lot worse before it gets better."

Eleven

Ben had been right. It did get worse. For the next two days the phone rang off the hook. And rather than dispersing, the mob of media out front only grew in size. And as morbid as it was, she couldn't stop herself from sitting in front of the television watching the cable entertainment shows, seeing what new information they had dredged up about her. Or in some cases, fabricated.

By far the lowest, most humiliating point had been when she'd read that her own mother had accepted ten thousand dollars for an exclusive interview. She didn't doubt that her stepfather had fueled that fire. There was a photograph of them together, standing on the porch of their broken down shack of a house in Utah. The five years since she'd last seen them hadn't been a friend to either. Her stepdad was still a fat disgusting pig and her mother looked old, tired and used up. And sadly, ninety percent of the exclusive interview was based on lies and half truths. She hadn't been an angel in her youth, but they had painted her as a strung out sex-crazed juvenile delinquent.

"We could sue for slander," Ben suggested, but honestly, she didn't see the point. True or not true, the information was out there and there was no taking it back. Ever. A lawsuit wouldn't stop people from believing, and it's not as if they could get damages from a couple who had nothing. She wouldn't even want to.

And when she was sure they had reached the absolute rock bottom and things could not possibly get any worse, any more complicated, they did.

She and Ben were in the dining room eating dinner when the doorbell rang.

Ben was already at the end of his patience and struggling to hang on. "They have a lot of nerve coming to the door."

Mrs. Smith emerged from the kitchen. "Would you like me to take care of it?"

Ben threw his napkin down onto his plate. "No. I think it's time I gave them a piece of my mind."

Tess cringed, knowing this was all her fault. Her relationship with him, the existence of the baby, was the only thing they were interested in.

Ben got up and headed for the foyer. She could hear the angry thud of his footsteps on the marble floor, the squeak of the hinges as he flung the front door open.

She waited for the shouting and the cursing, but what she heard was a long pause, then a baffled sounding, "*Mom,* what are you doing here?"

Oh boy, could this get any messier? Ben's mother had flown all the way from Europe, probably to drive Tess away. As any good mother would considering what the press had been reporting.

Tess stood at the far end of the foyer, trying to make herself invisible. Ben just looked stunned.

"Oh my goodness, what a dreadful mess!" his mother chirped, waving a hand dramatically in her face. She had no idea how true that was. "Now I remember why I got out of the entertainment business. Nasty people those reporters."

"Mom, what are you doing here? I told you it isn't a good time."

She gave him a patient smile. "It looks to me as though this is the perfect time."

As much as Tess would have liked to be able to tell herself Ben's mom looked like a normal everyday person, she didn't. She looked young and gorgeous and glamorous—like the movie star she'd been. And Tess felt like an ugly duckling.

Then Mrs. Adams looked around, her eyes screeching to a halt on Tess, as though she'd just realized someone else was standing there with them.

"Is this her?" she asked Ben.

"Mom, this is Tess. Tess, this is my mom."

Mrs. Adams swept across the foyer, gliding with

such smooth grace, Tess could swear her feet never hit the ground. She took Tess by the shoulders and looked her up and down. Tess waited for her to shove her away in disgust or possibly spit on her shoes. Instead, tears welled in her eyes and she yanked Tess, very unladylike, into a crushing hug.

Tess was so shocked that for a minute she forgot to breathe, and when she finally did, a cloud of flowery perfume filled her lungs. Over her shoulder, Tess saw Ben cringe.

"Oh, Benji, she's *adorable!*"

Benji? Tess mouthed the nickname back to him and Ben rolled his eyes.

Mrs. Adams held her at arm's length again, the tears hovering just inside her lids, as if they knew better than to spill over and mar her perfectly applied makeup.

Tess felt like a new family pet, a fuzzy little puppy they could housebreak and teach tricks. And she didn't get it. The tabloids had painted her as some moneygrubbing harlot. Mrs. Adams was acting as if she were happy to meet Tess.

"When are you due, sweetheart?" Mrs. Adams asked her, her grip on her arms not loosening.

It had been so long since anyone actually asked about the pregnancy, it took a minute for Tess to realize she meant her due date. "September nineteenth."

She let out a gasp. "Mine is the thirtieth! Maybe it will be born then!"

Eleven days late? God, she hoped not. She already felt like an elephant.

She turned to her son. "Benji, why didn't you tell us. Didn't you think we would want to know about our grandchild?"

"I planned to," Ben said, but Tess had the feeling it was a lie. He didn't want his parents to know about the baby. He didn't want them to get attached.

"Mom, why don't we get you settled in, then we'll talk?"

"That's a wonderful idea," his mother said, gently touching her shellacked hair. "I must look a fright after the long trip. Mrs. Smith, could you please have my bags taken to the guest suite?"

Mrs. Smith shot Ben a questioning look.

"I'm sorry, Mom, but the guest suite is occupied. You'll have to take a spare bedroom."

"Who's staying in the guest suite?" she asked.

"Tess is," Ben said, bracing for the questions that would follow.

He didn't have to wait long.

"Why on earth is she staying in the guest suite?"

This was going to be tough for her to understand. His mom, the hopeless romantic, would undoubtedly be very disappointed in him.

"We'll talk later," he told her. He would explain everything the minute he'd decided what to say.

He opened the front door to get the bags from the porch, and found five *enormous* cases sitting there. His mom tended to overpack, but this was ridiculous. "Um, how long were you planning on staying?"

"Well, until the baby is born, of course! Did you think I would miss the birth of my first grandchild?"

Ben cringed. This was worse than he'd thought. "What about Dad? Doesn't he mind you being gone so long?"

She waved a hand at him. "Oh, you know your father."

What was that supposed to mean?

"If I'd known you were coming, I could have prepared." As in he would have told her to stay in Europe.

"Didn't Mrs. Smith tell you I was coming?" his mom asked.

Mrs. Smith had talked to her? He looked over to his housekeeper who was trying hard not to look guilty. Peculiar that he was only hearing about this now.

"It must have slipped my mind," she said.

That was a lie, and he knew it. She had a mind like a steel trap. She never forgot anything.

He turned to his mom. "We'll get you settled in, then we'll talk. Mrs. Smith, when my mom has everything she needs, please come see me in my office."

She nodded, then led Mrs. Adams up the stairs.

"I get the feeling someone is in big trouble," Tess said from behind him.

"Yes," he agreed, turning to her. "Someone certainly is. I can't believe Mrs. Smith didn't warn me she was coming."

"This is bad, huh?"

"It's not the end of the world, but it is going to complicate things."

"If she asks me what's going on, what should I tell her?"

He didn't want Tess telling her anything, not until he'd decided exactly how much he wanted his parents to know. Besides, it wasn't fair to dump any of this on her. It was his responsibility. "You don't have to tell her anything. Just leave the explanations to me."

"You wanted to see me?"

Ben looked up to find Mrs. Smith standing in his office doorway. "Come in and shut the door."

She shut the door and walked stiffly to his desk. She had to know he would be furious with her for this.

"What has gotten into you? Why didn't you tell me the minute she called? I could have smoothed this over. You know how I felt about her coming here."

She gave him her usual belligerent, down-the-nose stare. "I was only thinking of your best interests."

"How is this my *best interests?*"

"That baby is her grandchild. She deserves to know it. Besides I can see how happy you are when you're with Tess. Even if you're too stubborn to admit it."

"How I feel about Tess is completely beside the point." He rubbed his eyes with the heels of his palms. "I have to figure out a way to explain why they can't be a part of the baby's life."

"There's no reason they can't be grandparents to this child."

"There's one damned good reason," he said hotly.

"How will they explain it once he's older? Why it's okay to see his grandparents, but not his own father?"

"If you feel as thoughs you've done nothing wrong, and your actions are justified, why would you care what the child thinks?"

He hated when she cornered him with logic. She always had this way of making him question himself, when he knew deep down he was making the right decision.

"Maybe this is something you should have considered before," she said.

"Before what? Before I accidentally got her pregnant? Despite what you believe, this was not an easy decision for me to make."

"I only want what's best for you, Ben."

"Which means what?"

"It means Tess is best for you. You need her, and you need this baby. You need them almost as much as they need you."

He shook his head. "I can't go through that again."

"You don't have a choice. It's done. That girl is having your baby and there is nothing you can do to change that."

"Everyone has a choice, and I've made mine." He stood. "Now if you'll excuse me, I need to go speak with my mother. I have to figure out a way to fix this mess. To get her back on a plane and out of California."

"You can't run forever," she said.

"Oh, yeah. Watch me."

Twelve

"**Y**ou should have told me," Ben's mom said, after he spent twenty humiliating minutes explaining the situation. It was bad enough having to admit to his mother that he had had a one night stand. But when she started in on him about the virtues of safe sex, he'd had to explain that they had practiced safe sex. Unfortunately there had been a condom malfunction.

"Why do I get the impression you weren't going to tell me at all?" she asked.

"No," he admitted. "If the press hadn't gotten a hold of the story, I probably wouldn't have."

He could see she was disappointed, and he was sorry for that, but that was just life. He had spent most of his childhood feeling disappointment of one form or another. He owed her a little bit of misery.

She shook her head sadly. "I raised you better than this."

"*You* raised me? Are you kidding?" It was probably due to the stress from the media coverage, but all the bottled up disappointment and feelings of indignant anger he'd buried during his childhood welled to the surface. "*You* didn't raise me at all. Mrs. Smith did. You were too busy being a star to give a damn about what was happening to me."

He hadn't meant to be cruel, but the words just sort of flew out. Maybe he'd needed to say them for a long time.

Too long.

She didn't even have the decency to look wounded. "Well then, don't make the same mistakes I did. Be there for your child."

Her words stung. And the fact that she didn't bother to deny it surprised him.

"This baby will be well taken care of. He'll have the best of everything."

"That obviously wasn't good enough for you, was it?"

Ouch. Direct hit. But this was different.

"Do you think he won't notice that he doesn't have a father?"

He'd thought about that, and he hated it, but there was nothing he could do about it. "Maybe it would be best if you just go home."

"I'm not leaving, Ben. I may have been a lousy mother, but I'm going to be the best damned grandma you'll ever meet. So you might as well get used to the idea."

"And what about Dad?"

"What about him?"

"How does he feel about you being gone for three months?"

"To tell you the truth, I don't think he cares."

Ben gave his mom a disbelieving look. His father had an ego as wide and deep as the Grand Canyon. He lived to be doted on and pampered. It would only be a matter of time before he demanded she come home and pay attention to him.

"I didn't want to bother you with this, but you should probably know that your father and I are getting divorced."

She said it so calmly, it took a second for the meaning of the words to hit home. "*Divorced?* What happened?"

"He's trading me in for a younger model. Literally. She was on the cover of the swimsuit issue last year. Thirty-eight years younger than him. The poor thing doesn't know what she's getting into."

His world felt as if it had been flipped upside down and dropped on its head. He wasn't naive. He'd heard rumors that his dad had flings with his costars. Ben had never asked if it was true, and neither his mom nor his dad had ever brought it up. And thank God for that, because frankly, he didn't want to know.

But his parents had been together for almost thirty-five years. How could his dad just up and leave her?

And why didn't she seem all that disturbed by it. He would have thought she'd be devastated.

"When did this happen?"

"After Christmas."

"That was months ago! Why didn't you tell me?"

"That isn't something you tell someone over the phone."

Aw hell, now it made sense. Now he understood why his mom kept calling and asking to visit. She'd needed to talk to him, and probably just plain needed him, and he kept blowing her off.

"I'm sorry."

She patted his shoulder. "So, as you can imagine, your father most definitely does not need me, meaning I'm in no rush to get back. In fact, I may never go back. I may just stay here with you in California. You have the room."

That had to be a joke. For thirty-two years she all but ignores him, now she wants to move into his house? And what was he supposed to do? Ask her to leave. Tell her he didn't want her around. He may have had a lot of pent-up hostility toward her, but he didn't want to hurt her feelings. Especially after what his father had done to her.

This was nuts.

"Now shoo," she said. "I have to unpack and fix my face. Then I'd like a tour of this lovely house."

The best Ben could do, as his mother shoved him

out the door and into the hall, was smile and pretend like everything was normal. When he had the distinct feeling life would never be *normal* again.

Tess walked slowly through the garden, stopping here and there to inhale a bloom, the sun warming her skin. She tried to convince herself she was just out there enjoying the weather—even if that meant getting caught on film by some elusive photographer's telephoto lens—when the truth was, she was hiding. She didn't want to run into Ben's mom, and possibly have to explain her side of the story.

She didn't have a clue what to say. Her face was plastered on every gossip rag, her entire life—complete with juicy lies for added flavor—printed in black and white for the world to read.

Although she couldn't help being curious about what Ben had told his mom, and how she felt about him not wanting the baby.

"Tess!"

Tess turned to see Mrs. Adams gliding toward her down the path, arm waving wildly. Tess cursed under her breath. She couldn't exactly outrun her. She had no choice but to stop and wait.

"Mrs. Smith said I would probably find you out here," she said breathlessly as she caught up.

Tess would have to remember to thank Mrs. Smith. Maybe a garter snake in her bed.

"It is okay if I call you Tess, dear?"

"Of course," Tess told her. She was surprised she

would even ask. She would have expected something a bit more colorful, like Harlot or Tramp.

"Phew!" Mrs. Adams waved a hand in front of her face. "It is warm out here, isn't it?" If she was overheated, it didn't show. She looked cool and dry in her rose colored blouse and white slacks. Tess doubted people like Ben's mom even had sweat glands.

"It is warm," Tess agreed, knowing she probably hadn't come out here to talk about the weather. There was more coming.

Just smile and make nice and agree with everything she says. Grovel if necessary.

They walked slowly, side by side. Well, Tess waddled and Mrs. Adams glided.

"I recall being hot all the time when I was pregnant with Benji. And sick, right up until the day he was born. That's why I never had more children." She waved her hand, as if she could swat the unpleasant thought away like a pesky bug. "I think that's why Benji always wanted a family so badly. Because he felt lonely growing up. His father and I were gone far too much."

Ben had wanted a family. She'd just come along a little too late.

That shouldn't have hurt so much. She shouldn't have felt so cheated. But she did. Somewhere deep down, as often as she denied it, she still wanted the fairy tale. The happily ever after.

"I only hope that you don't hold this against him. He's a good man, Tess."

"I know he is." If she didn't know any better, she would think Ben's mom wanted him and Tess together.

"It's been terribly difficult for him since he lost Jeanette," she went on. "You might not realize this, but your being here has helped him."

Tess swallowed hard. "I take it you two have… talked."

"Yes, we've talked. He explained the situation. He's quite convinced he's doing the right thing."

"You don't agree?"

She laughed. "Heavens, no! I think he's being an ass. That's my grandbaby you're carrying. That makes you a part of this family."

Tears burned behind Tess' eyes. She'd never expected Ben's mom to accept her into their family. "I guess I thought…well, the things that you probably read about me…"

She stopped abruptly and took Tess firmly by the shoulders. "Dear, let's get something straight. I was in the entertainment business a long time. Long enough to know that ninety-nine percent of what you read in the tabloids is fabrication, and the other one percent is usually only half-right." She let out a long, exasperated sigh, laying a hand gently across Tess's belly. "If I live to be two hundred, I will never understand men and their egos. My son tells me I can never see my grandchild and thinks I'm just going to nod and agree. He's like his father in that respect. He left me, you know. My husband. For a twenty-year-old supermodel."

Holy—why was she telling Tess this? "I'm so sorry." She didn't know what else *to* say.

"I'm better off without him," she said bravely, then her lips began to quiver.

Uh-oh.

She dragged in a shaky breath and forced a smile. "Are you okay?"

"I'm fine," she said. "Just fine." Then buried her face in her hands and dissolved into tears.

For a second, Tess was too stunned to react. What had happened to the larger-than-life, confident superstar? And what was she supposed to do? Stand there and watch while the woman fell apart?

She did the only thing she could, what she would want someone to do if she were having an emotional melt down, she wrapped her arms around Ben's mom and hugged her.

"I'm sorry," Ben's mom said, the words drowned out by a sob.

"It's okay," Tess said, patting her back. She led Ben's mom to a bench and sat beside her. She dug a clean tissue out of her pocket and pushed it into her hand.

Mrs. Adams sniffled daintily and dabbed her eyes. "I'm not naive. I knew he'd had flings over the years. But I loved him so much I pretended not to notice, even though it broke my heart every time he came home smelling like another woman's perfume. But he did come home. No matter who he was sleeping with, he was still mine at the end of the day."

"I'm so sorry," Tess said, rubbing her shoulder.

She couldn't imagine loving someone so much she would tolerate infidelity. Ben's mom was gorgeous and famous. Why would she put up with that if she could probably have any other man in the world?

Because she was human, Tess realized. Not a larger-than-life icon. Today she was just a lonely and confused woman who needed a shoulder to cry on.

"On top of everything else I'm going through menopause," she said, fresh tears rolling down her cheeks. "Anyone who tells you it's not that horrible is full of bunk. I feel so *old*."

"You don't look old. And I have no idea how you can cry without your makeup running. Mine would be all over my face."

"Waterproof mascara. One hundred and twenty bucks a tube and worth every penny." With a wistful sigh, she reached up and touched Tess's cheek. It was such a gentle, motherly gesture, Tess felt her heart swell. "Just look at that gorgeous skin. I used to have skin like that. So youthful. I don't dare go without makeup these days. I look ghastly without my face on."

"You're beautiful," Tess said.

"My plastic surgeon thanks you." At Tess's surprised look she said, "It's no secret that I've had work done, for all the good it's done me. I should have just let myself grow old gracefully. You think you're turning the biological clock off, then you realize you've really only hit the snooze button. But enough about me. Tell me about your pregnancy."

"What would you like to know?"

Excitement sparked in her youthful eyes. *"Everything."*

It was Tess's turn to get weepy. It was stupid, but besides her doctor, not a single person had asked her about her pregnancy. She'd been dying to tell someone. *Anyone.*

She told Ben's mom *everything,* down to the last little detail. They sat outside in the garden for hours, talking as if they'd been acquainted for years. Despite being from opposite ends of the social spectrum, they bonded out there among the flowers. They became friends.

She knew, without a doubt, even if she couldn't rely on Ben to be there for her and the baby, his mom would never let her down. It made her feel a little less lonely.

Things got very weird after his mom arrived. Or maybe things were normal, which for Ben was unusual.

They coexisted together like a happy family, which, ironically, is exactly what he'd told Tess wouldn't happen. Unfortunately he wasn't the one calling the shots anymore. His mom had come in and completely taken over.

He'd seen more of her in the past two months than he had the last twenty years. She and Tess were practically attached at the hip. They took long walks and went shopping together, and his mom even went with Tess for her seventh and eighth month checkups. She planned to be there for the birth, so they began taking Lamaze classes together once a week.

Sometimes the two of them would sit for hours and just talk. Not only could he not imagine what they could possibly have in common, but he was also sure they would have eventually run out of things to talk about.

His mom had even managed to defuse the situation with the press. They had accosted her and Tess in town. Someone shoved a microphone in his mom's face and asked, "How do you feel about becoming a grandmother?"

His mom slipped her arm through Tess's and gave the camera crews a bright, genuine smile. "My husband and I couldn't be more thrilled. We adore Tess. Now if you gentlemen will excuse us, we have shopping to do."

She always had been great at working a crowd.

Ben gave up trying to stop it. In part because he could see that it was useless, and another part of him was actually enjoying having his mom around. Enjoying, for the first time in his life—and probably the last—the feeling of close family.

Although sometimes he could swear his mom liked Tess more than him.

But it couldn't last. After the baby was born, which was a mere three weeks away now, they couldn't pretend to be a happy family anymore. Although he had the sneaking suspicion that when the time came, he was going to be the odd man out.

He would be alone and Tess would have his family. Even Mrs. Smith was making noises like she might stay with Tess for a few months until she got settled into her new condo.

He might have been angry, or even hurt, but Tess was so happy lately. One evening after they had made love, she told him that for the first time in her life, she felt loved. She thanked him for sharing his mom with her.

He'd begun having those thoughts again, like maybe there was a way to make this work.

Then the other shoe fell. In fact, they *both* did. Ben was in his office working when his mother burst through the door, her face white as death.

"Tess fell!"

He died a thousand deaths in the three seconds it took him to jump from his chair and follow her to the base of the stairs where Tess was sitting on the marble floor clutching her left ankle. Mrs. Smith crouched beside her.

There was no blood, she wasn't unconscious. Nothing looked broken. She was okay.

His heart was hammering so hard and he felt so light-headed with relief he nearly joined her on the floor. "What happened?"

"My bad ankle," Tess said. "It gave out on me when I was walking down the stairs."

"You should be more careful," he snapped. He didn't mean to. He *never* meant to get mad at her when what she really needed was comfort. He just did.

Suddenly everyone was looking at him like he was an ogre.

It wasn't an unfair assessment.

"Gee, Ben, you think?" Tess snapped back. But she looked more hurt than angry. "It's probably the extra weight and water retention irritating it. There's not much I can do about that."

"Do you think you can walk?" Mrs. Smith asked.

"I think s—" She gasped and folded in half. "Oh!"

Ben went from relieved to petrified in an instant. "What's wrong?"

"Pain in my stomach," she gasped. "You want to blame that on me too?"

He'd definitely deserved that.

Ben's mom shot him a distressed look. Even Mrs. Smith looked worried.

It passed after a few seconds. She sat up and said, "That was weird."

"Are you all right?" his mom asked.

She nodded. "I think so."

"Let's get you up off the floor." His mom shot him a look, but he just stood there. He knew he should help, but he couldn't move.

This was all his fault. He should have never let her climb the stairs alone. He should have insisted she use the service elevator behind the kitchen. If she lost the baby because of his carelessness…

She wasn't going to lose the baby. He was just overreacting again. She was fine.

The women helped Tess to her feet and Ben saw her wince when she put weight on her ankle.

"Can you walk on it?" Mrs. Smith asked.

"I think so." She started to take a step then let out a startled gasp and doubled over again, clutching her belly. "Ow! That hurts!"

She couldn't possibly be in labor. It was too early. She still had three weeks to go.

"Maybe we should take you to the doctor," Ben said, waiting for the women to say not to worry, Tess was fine. Random stomach pain was completely normal.

It's what he desperately *needed* to hear.

Instead, when Tess looked up at him, there was fear in her eyes. "That might not be a bad idea."

Thirteen

Tess lay in bed, the television on, flipping mindlessly through the channels. There were a million of them, and not a damned thing on she wanted to watch.

She didn't know how much more of this she could take.

After her fall, the doctor had confined her to bed. Her ankle was only twisted, but her blood pressure had been elevated, so she was ordered to stay off her feet for the duration of her pregnancy. Two weeks later she had a serious case of cabin fever.

Ben's mom stayed with her most of the time, and some evenings Mrs. Smith came in and played cards with them, or watched a movie. Sometimes they just sat around—or in Tess's case lay around—talking.

Ben's mom never ran out of stories to tell. She could always make Tess smile.

Ben was another story altogether. Tess knew that her accident would be a defining moment in their relationship. He would either be so relieved she and the baby were okay, he would realize what a fool he'd been and they would live happily ever after, or this would freak him out to the point that he shut her out completely.

Unfortunately, it was the latter.

Ben hadn't been in to see her the entire two weeks she'd been off her feet. He wouldn't even go into the examining room with her at the hospital while the doctor saw her. It was as if she didn't exist anymore.

As hard as she had tried not to, she'd let herself believe there was a chance with Ben. Things had been going so well that she'd had hope. How many times had she told herself she expected no more than he was willing to give? Only now, when she was faced with the limitation of that, did she realize it had been a lie. She wanted it all.

She probably should have been hurt and rejected, but the truth was, she just felt numb. And foolish.

Foolish for letting herself fall in love.

At least she still had Ben's mom to keep her company. She was Tess's family now. The mother that Tess had never had.

There was a soft knock at the bedroom door and Ben's mom popped her head in. "Are you awake?"

"I'm awake," Tess said, shutting off the television and tossing the remote aside. She wished she could sleep more. She wished she could drift off and wake up when the baby was due. "Awake and in danger of dying from boredom."

"I brought your lunch," she said, stepping in the room holding a tray.

"I'm not very hungry." She was never hungry anymore. She felt tired all the time, too, but couldn't seem to sleep for more than a couple of hours at a time. She was probably depressed, and just too numb to realize it.

Ben's mom set the tray on the nightstand. "How are you feeling?"

Tess shrugged. "My back is still bothering me, but otherwise I'm okay I guess."

"I wanted to talk to you about something." Ben's mom sat on the edge of the bed. "My husband called me last night."

"Really?" Tess sat up. "What did he say?"

"He said he made a terrible mistake and he wants me to come home. The thing with the model only lasted a few weeks but he's been too ashamed to call. He says he's been miserable without me."

As hard as she tried to hide how much she missed Ben's dad, Tess knew deep down she was miserable, too. "What do you think?"

"I think he sounds like he means it. Or maybe I just want to think that. I told him that before I would even consider reconciling with him, a lot of things would have to change. The infidelity would have to stop for one thing. I deserve better."

"Good for you." She was right, she did deserve better. And so did Tess—better than what Ben could offer her. Only problem was, she didn't think she could find anyone better for her, anyone she could love more than Ben. She didn't even feel like trying. Maybe she would feel differently later, after the baby was born and she got her life back together.

"He booked us rooms at a resort in Acapulco, so we can spend some time alone and sort things out. He wants me to meet him there tomorrow."

"Are you going to go?"

"I told him I'd think about it and call him back today. He seems genuinely sorry, but I hate the thought of leaving you. You need me here."

The thought of Ben's mom leaving broke Tess's heart, but her marriage was at stake. That was definitely more important.

She forced a smile. "I think you should go. I'll be fine."

"If I did go, I would make sure I was back a few days before the baby is due. I promised to be there with you, and I won't let you down."

What if something happened and she didn't make it back in time? Tess would have to go through it alone. The idea made her sick inside, but she wouldn't let it show. She couldn't be selfish. This was something Ben's mom needed to do. "I know you won't."

"I tried to talk to him again," Ben's mom said, and by *him* Tess knew she meant Ben. "He just won't listen."

Well, if nothing else, Ben was consistent. "Thanks for trying."

"Maybe he'll come around. Maybe after the baby is born—"

"I can't let myself believe that. If I do, and he doesn't…" A knot of emotion settled in her throat and wouldn't let the rest of the words out.

Ben's mom put her arms around Tess and hugged her. "I just don't understand it. I know he loves you."

The worst part was, she did, too. But sometimes love just wasn't enough.

Ben stared blindly at his computer screen, at the game of solitaire he wasn't really playing. He couldn't sleep. Just like last night. And the night before that, and the night before that. He hadn't had a decent night's sleep in two weeks, since the day Tess fell. And he felt as though he might never again.

He hated what he must have been doing to her. If she felt even half as tortured and sick inside as he did, she had to be miserable. It was like losing his family all over again. He had tried a million times to walk down the hall to her suite, but he could never make it all the way to the door. Every time something stopped him.

"Ben?"

Tess's voice. She was standing in his office doorway. He looked at the clock and saw that it was after midnight.

The doctor had told her to stay off her feet. She shouldn't even be out of bed.

"What are you doing down here?" He didn't mean to sound angry, but he couldn't seem to stop himself. He had to hold on to his anger and grief, or he would wind up pulling her into his arms and holding her. And that wouldn't be fair to Tess.

"Would you mind calling me a cab?" she asked, her voice sounding small and strained.

"What for?"

"I need to go to the hospital." She stepped into his office, and as she drew nearer, into the lamplight, he could see her skin was pale and her forehead damp with perspiration.

"What's wrong?"

"Nothing is wrong. I'm in labor."

"You can't be, you're not due for another week." He realized how dumb that sounded the second the words left his mouth.

"I thought so, too," she said. "Apparently the baby is ready now."

"Are you sure?"

"Incredibly sure."

He just stood there. He couldn't seem to make his feet move. He knew this day was going to come. But why did it have to be today? He wasn't ready for this.

Though he didn't think standing here like an idiot was going to stop it.

She clutched her belly. "Unless you want to deliver this baby yourself, I would call now."

"How close together are your contractions?"

"Every three or four minutes."

That got his attention. *"Three minutes?* How long have you been in labor?"

"I guess since this morning."

"This morning?" She couldn't be serious. "Why didn't you say something sooner?"

"It was all in my back, but I've had a backache for weeks. I didn't actually figure out that it was labor, until about ten minutes ago when my water broke."

His stomach dropped out. "Jesus, your water broke, too?"

"Would you please stop yelling at me!" she shouted, then her eyes went wide and she gasped a breath, clutching the edge of his desk. "Oh boy, here comes another one."

Tess gritted her teeth and tried to remember to breathe as the contraction hit her with the force and velocity of an express train. The pain just kept building and building until she didn't think she could stand it anymore, until tears were leaking out of her eyes. They said it would hurt, but never in her worst nightmare had she dreamed it would be this painful.

After what felt like hours, the pain finally began to ease. This was *so* not fun. This kid could just forget about natural birth. She wanted drugs. Lots and lots of drugs. And siblings were completely out of the question.

She looked up and saw that Ben was just standing there. His baffled expression might have been amusing in any other situation, but right now all she wanted to do was reach inside him, yank his spine out, stomp on it a couple million times and then set it on fire. Maybe then he would have at least a clue how damned much this hurt.

"I really need that cab," she said through gritted teeth.

"Somehow I don't think you have time to wait for a cab. Where is your bag?"

"By the stairs."

"I'll help you to the car."

He probably thought she did this on purpose, so he would have to drive her.

"Maybe Mrs. Smith could drive me."

"She doesn't drive at night." He led her to the garage, grabbing her bag as they passed the stairs.

"I'm sorry."

"Sorry for what?" he asked.

"That you have to do this."

He didn't answer, but she knew that he was sorry, too. He didn't want to go through this. But he would because he knew she needed him. He got her into the car just as the next contraction hit. They were coming even closer now, and she was beginning to feel pressure where the baby's head was coming down.

"Drive fast," she told him as he climbed in.

He started his car, peeled out of the garage and roared through the gates to the street. This was not the way she'd imagined this happening. She was supposed to have more time. Ben's mom was supposed to be here. Suddenly she couldn't remember a single thing she'd learned in class.

She felt so useless. Her body was doing all these off-the-wall things and she had no control. What if something went wrong? What if something happened to the baby?

She needed someone to tell her what to do.

"I can't do this," she told Ben. "I changed my mind. I don't want to have a baby."

"I think it's a little late for that, sweetheart."

"I'm scared."

He took her hand and squeezed it. "Everything is going to be okay."

But it wouldn't be. Not everything. They'd reached the end of the road. *Everything* would never be okay again.

The drive to the hospital was nothing but a blur of pain. Every bump they hit in the road, every turn he took, rocked through her body like a catastrophic earthquake. Her entire midsection, front to back, felt like a gigantic exposed nerve. It was so all-encompassing that she couldn't even determine the point of origin anymore. It just hurt, sharp and stinging, and it hurt *everywhere.*

Her only comfort was the reassuring squeeze of Ben's hand.

He drove *way* too fast, with only one hand on the wheel, and she was pretty sure he ran two or three red lights. Thank God it was the middle of the night and no one was on the road, and the hospital was only ten minutes away.

"You can just drop me off here," she told him when they pulled up to the emergency room doors. An orderly met them at the car with a wheelchair. She had just managed to slide into it when another contraction hit swift and intense. Every time she thought it couldn't possibly get any worse, it somehow managed to. It made sense now why she was an only child. How could a second pregnancy be anything but an accident? Who would want to go through this *twice?*

She could hear people talking around her, but through a haze of pain she couldn't focus on the words. She thought this one was just going to last forever, but it finally began to ease when they reached the elevator. Only then did it register that someone was holding her hand, and she looked up to see Ben standing beside her. "You're still here?"

"I'm still here."

And he wasn't leaving. Ben had no idea what he was doing, he only knew that he wasn't enough of a bastard to make her do this alone. He didn't let himself think about the repercussions. All he knew was that he loved her too much to leave her. It would probably be the hardest thing he'd ever had to do in his life, but he owed her that much.

The grip on his hand snapped like a vise, and he knew she was having another contraction. He stroked her hair and talked to her in a low, soothing voice. He remembered enough from his classes with Jeanette to remind her to focus and breathe.

He had a bad feeling that if they didn't get her to a room soon she was going to have this kid in the elevator. How long did it take to ride up four floors for God's sake?

Finally the bell tinged and the doors dragged slowly open. The orderly led them down the hall to Labor and Delivery. Next came the nurses, and a million questions he should have known the answers to. Everyone was calling him *Dad* and acting as if he was supposed to be there and he played along because it was the only thing he could do.

They barely had time to get her to a room, into a gown and prepped. In the whirlwind of activity, he stayed right beside her, talking her through it.

"I want drugs," Tess told the nurse who was taking her blood pressure. Then she turned to Ben and begged, "Tell them to give me drugs."

Ben looked at the doctor but she shook her head. "No time. She's fully effaced and dilated and the baby is coming down. Whenever you're ready, Tess, start pushing."

After a couple of false starts, Tess seemed to get the hang of it. Ben helped her sit up and counted out the seconds while she pushed, finally feeling as if he were doing some good.

Considering the force of her contractions, he expected the baby to shoot out like a bullet but it was slow going. He wiped the sweat from her forehead, fed her ice chips when she rested, watched in awe as she worked diligently to push the baby out. In his life he'd never loved or respected a woman more than he did Tess.

"The baby is crowning," the doctor said after forty minutes or so.

Ben didn't even stop to think about what he was doing. He just peered down to look and saw the top of the baby's head, covered with what looked like a lot of dark hair. It was the most amazing thing he had ever seen. "Oh my God. Tess, I can see the baby."

"One more big push," the doctor told her.

"I can't," Tess gasped. "I'm too tired."

"Look at me," Ben said, and she looked up at him, her eyes glassy. Two hours ago, he couldn't have been less ready for this baby to be born, now it was all he wanted. "You can do this. One more push and it will be all over."

She took a deep breath and he could see her gathering all her strength, giving it everything she had. Eyes closed in concentration, she bore down one last time and the baby popped out, slippery and squirmy with a full head of dark hair. Just like his.

"It's a girl." The doctor rolled her onto Tess's stomach and suctioned out her mouth.

A girl. A daughter.

He and Tess had a daughter.

She was small and pink and already exercising her lungs. And more beautiful that anything he had ever laid his eyes on.

Tess touched her. Her tiny little arms and legs, her fingers and toes. "Look at her, Ben. She's perfect."

The baby stopped crying and turned her head toward the sound of Tess's voice. She looked up at them both with bright, curious blue eyes. Intelligent eyes.

Ben fell instantly and completely in love with her.

It was so ridiculous to him that he had actually thought he could stop himself from loving her. The second she came screaming into the world she was his. Totally and absolutely a part of him.

He hadn't cried since the third grade, not even when he lost his son, but he could feel actual tears burning in his eyes.

"I am so sorry," he told Tess. "I don't know what I was thinking. How could I have not known how much I would love her?"

She reached up and wiped the tears from his cheeks.

"I love you, Tess."

"I love you, too."

The nurse took the baby away long enough to weigh, measure and clean her up—which felt like an eternity to Tess—then she wrapped her in a pink receiving blanket and brought her back. Gradually the room cleared until it was just Tess and Ben and the baby.

Their baby.

She was going to grow up happy, with a mommy and a daddy and grandparents to love her. A real family. She would never know just how lucky she was, and that was exactly the way Tess intended to keep it.

Ben sat on the bed beside her, gazing down at the little bundle in his arms. Tess had nursed her for a while, and Ben had been holding her ever since. And as much as Tess wanted a turn, she knew Ben needed her more right now. They had years and years to share her. To watch her grow and change.

"She looks just like you," he said, playing with her tiny little fingers.

"Your mom will be so disappointed she missed this."

He shrugged. "So she'll be here for the next one."

She shot him a questioning look.

"I know I don't deserve a second chance, but if you let me, I swear I'll make it up to you."

She just smiled. "You already have."

All this time she'd been wrong. Fairy tales could be real—if you just had faith. And in her story, the dark, enchanted castle was now filled with light and laughter and new life. And the prince had been set free from his curse by the love of a maiden.

The miniature one snuggled in his arms.

* * * * *

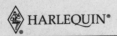

HARLEQUIN®

American ROMANCE®

American Beauties

SORORITY SISTERS, FRIENDS FOR LIFE

Michele Dunaway

THE MARRIAGE CAMPAIGN

Campaign fund-raiser Lisa Meyer has worked
hard to be her own boss and will let nothing—
especially romance—interfere with her success.
To Mark Smith, Lisa is the perfect candidate for
him to spend his life with. But if she lets herself
fall for Mark, will she lose all she's worked for?
Or will she have a future that's more than
she's ever dreamed of?

On sale August 2006

Also watch for:

THE WEDDING SECRET
On sale December 2006

NINE MONTHS NOTICE
On sale April 2007

Available wherever Harlequin books are sold.

**Hidden in the secrets of antiquity,
lies the unimagined truth...**

Introducing

a brand-new line filled with mystery
and suspense, action and adventure,
and a fascinating look into history.

And it all begins with DESTINY.

In a sealed crypt in
France, where the
terrifying legend of
the beast of Gevaudan
begins to unravel,
Annja Creed discovers
a stunning artifact
that will seal her destiny.

*Available every other
month starting
July 2006, wherever
you buy books.*

GRA1

Stability is highly overrated....

Dana Logan's world had always revolved around her children. Now they're all grown up and don't seem to need anything she's able to give them. Struggling to find her new identity, Dana realizes that it's about time for her to get "off her rocker" and begin a new life!

Off Her Rocker

by Jennifer Archer

HN53
Available August 2006
TheNextNovel.com

HARLEQUIN
Next

COMING NEXT MONTH

#1741 MARRIAGE TERMS—Barbara Dunlop
The Elliotts
Seducing his ex-wife was the perfect way to settle the score, until the Elliott millionaire realized *he* was the one being seduced.

#1742 EXPECTING THUNDER'S BABY—
Sheri WhiteFeather
The Trueno Brides
A reckless affair leads to an unplanned pregnancy. But will they take another chance on love?

#1743 THE BOUGHT-AND-PAID-FOR WIFE—
Bronwyn Jameson
Secret Lives of Society Wives
She'd been his father's trophy wife and was now a widow. How could he dare make her his own?

#1744 BENDING TO THE BACHELOR'S WILL—
Emilie Rose
Trust Fund Affairs
She agreed to buy the wealthy tycoon at a charity bachelor auction as a favor, never expecting she'd gain so much in the bargain.

#1745 IAN'S ULTIMATE GAMBLE—Brenda Jackson
He'll stop at nothing to protect his casino, even partaking in a passionate escapade. But who will win this game of seduction?

#1746 BUNKING DOWN WITH THE BOSS—
Charlene Sands
A rich executive pretends to be a cowboy for the summer—and finds himself falling for his beautiful lady boss.